Praise for Jorrie Spencer's *Puma*

"Jorrie Spencer has to write some of the most original storylines I have ever come across. Just when I thought I had Puma figured out, it would go in a different direction and while I thought I knew what the story was going to entail, I didn't. Her suspenseful and well thought out writing kept me pretty much in suspense the entire time."

~ *Talia Ricci, Joyfully Reviewed*

Blue Ribbon Rating: 4.5 "PUMA is filled with mysteries to unfold. Ms. Spencer filled me with many emotions... Along with love and passion. It was a definite page turner..."

~ *Robin, Romance Junkies*

"...well-paced and the build-up towards the climax is done very nicely indeed. It's hard for me to say more without giving away things, so let me just say that I have a good time with this story."

~ *Mrs. Giggles*

Look for these titles by
Jorrie Spencer

Now Available:

Haven
Puma

The Strength Series
The Strength of the Pack (Book 1)
The Strength of the Wolf (Book 2)

Puma

Jorrie Spencer

A Samhain Publishing, Ltd. publication.

Samhain Publishing, Ltd.
577 Mulberry Street, Suite 1520
Macon, GA 31201
www.samhainpublishing.com

Puma
Copyright © 2009 by Jorrie Spencer
Print ISBN: 978-1-60504-339-5
Digital ISBN: 978-1-60504-221-3

Editing by Sasha Knight
Cover by Anne Cain

First Samhain Publishing, Ltd. electronic publication: October 2008
First Samhain Publishing, Ltd. print publication: August 2009

Dedication

For my mother.

Prologue

The male had made a home in this canyon, where his tawny fur blended with the sand, where the night could freeze you and the day bring your blood to a boil.

Werecougars, at least the few Callie knew of, usually chose to live farther north, but perhaps this one had been born here. After all, his animal counterpart, the cougar or puma, used to range throughout North America.

Callie placed one large paw after the other, intent on this trail, on her path forward, studiously ignoring the fact that she was being stalked by the one she sought. Exactly as they'd planned. She'd even screamed earlier to attract his attention. No male would ignore a female screaming.

If he was at all clever, he would stop and ask himself how she had arrived here so suddenly, alone. (For she was not alone.) But they weren't clever, these feral males. And while she sometimes felt a pang for their stupidity, it was generally overridden by the vicious and brutal way they slaughtered their prey. This one had killed six humans, including a five-year-old boy, and that she couldn't forgive.

He was close now, approaching from the right, and her heart rate sped up. Perhaps he wouldn't even be curious, perhaps he would simply attack. She almost hoped he would. Put an end to this job she had taken up four years ago and regretted every day since, and yet could not bring herself to leave.

She slowed down, willing him to pounce. She wouldn't mind a good fight, wouldn't mind going out in a blaze of glory. That was only her puma self speaking, but at the moment she didn't care.

Instead of an ambush though, the feral waited for her. Just before she could round the corner that would take them into the clear, he stepped in front of her and hissed, a question in the sound. She froze at the sight of him, her heart rising to her throat, for he was smaller than she was, which meant he was young, too young.

She didn't kill children, even murderous ones. She'd told Trey that when he'd hired her on.

Maybe this one is salvageable. Despite how this job had eroded all hope of saving one of her own kind, that thought took hold, and she could not turn away from it.

It wasn't her call to make. At this point, she had a protocol to follow, orders to carry out. She was the hired help.

But to find such a young male was a new development. To date, the killers had all been older, adult. Callie refused to treat this puma like the others. Trey would just have to deal with her executive decision to change the plans.

The male's tail wasn't even twitching, and he chirped, trying to speak to her. At least he was aware enough to realize she, like him, was a shapeshifter. A couple of the males, too far gone in their cougar heads, hadn't seemed to notice anything but that she was potential prey.

If she wanted to protect this one, she'd have to back up, lead him away from where they could pick him off with a long-range rifle. It wasn't quite the risk to her that it might have been, given his relatively small size. In a fight, she could hold her own, whereas a full-grown male would have been significantly larger and stronger than her.

She chirped back at him, but he didn't know what to make of the noise. This was frustrating. Werecougars had a repertoire of sounds, which also belonged to their animal kin, but given how badly most were socialized, they had difficulty knowing what the other meant. Right now, communication was extremely limited.

Callie stepped backwards, unwilling to take her eyes off him, but trying to lead him away from danger. The FBI had its pick of fantastic sharpshooters and cougars were relatively big targets.

She whistled at him to follow and he did. Careful, curious.

Trey was going to kill her—figuratively. She could just imagine him pitching a fit right now, in his silent, stoic way. Because she had most definitely veered off plan.

She heard the high-pitched whine and leapt, knocking the male to the ground before the bullet hit sand just beyond them. He snarled, swiping at her with his large paw, aggressive now that she'd initiated physical contact. So she rolled away, then ran, hoping he would give chase without catching her. The path she raced along narrowed and zigzagged into the low, parched bush. Anything to keep them both out of the sharpshooter's sight.

Her running would likely force his predator instincts to kick in so she slowed, though she was taking a chance, making herself vulnerable. The feral hit with his shoulder, knocking her sideways off her feet. *Shit.* His paw slashed down her belly and she expected to be gutted by the action, but unfathomably, he'd retracted his claws. While the swipe would be bruising, her skin remained intact.

So he wasn't in it for the kill. Something within her eased

as she rolled to her feet. She had always wanted to make contact with another werecougar, hadn't recognized how desperate she was to connect until she turned towards him.

Such a foolish move. She realized just how badly she had judged the male as teeth sank into her open throat.

The pain turned her world red, then black.

She woke human, lying on her back, her eyelids heavy, her thoughts slow. Though she had the wherewithal to think *I'm alive* and be surprised by it.

Her throat, he'd ripped it open. She moved to lift her hand and couldn't. Realized she was trapped, bound to a bed, and adrenaline surged through her, shocking her full awake. Opening her eyes, she gulped air—

"Easy." A hand came down on the arm she'd tried to move. "Just till you're conscious."

She blinked. Trey, her boss, was there, stroking her arm—he never stroked her arm—and speaking in soothing tones. How odd.

"You're not captive here. We had to restrain you so you could heal, that's all."

So her injuries warranted immobilization, and Trey's reassurance. *That* had never happened before.

"I've been waiting till you woke up and now I'm going to release your arms and legs, okay?"

"O—kay." Her voice felt rusty, but usable, despite the tenderness in her throat. She watched while he undid the plastic cuffs.

"Better?" he asked.

"Who are you and what have you done with my boss, Trey Walters?"

His mouth kicked up a little, his excuse for a smile. "He'll be back soon enough and then...there'll be hell to pay." These last words said with some steel behind them. However, his manner returned to that of the gentle imposter. "You need to feel better than this first." It was strange, his behavior. His normally cold eyes were actually warm. Kind of. For Trey Walters, stone-cold werewolf.

She'd always wanted to impress him and apparently getting herself almost killed had made some kind of impression, if not quite the one she'd been aiming for. She'd wanted to *accomplish* something, not get her throat ripped open.

Lifting her arms from her sides, she touched the IV taped to the back of her hand, tracing the plastic and needle with a finger.

"Listen. Leave that IV in."

"I don't need it." She was a puma. She healed herself. Medicine was for humans. But her protest wasn't as energetic as she would have liked. Weariness dragged at her in a way that was new and foreign to her.

"I happen to know you're a shifter, Callie. However, you basically died. We're going to play it safe." That steel returned. "Or I'll restrain you again."

"You're bluffing." This she mumbled as her eyelids drifted downwards. Was she on drugs? She struggled to speak, to ask him, hating the idea of drugs.

His palm came back to rest on her arm, a gesture to reassure her. It worked. A sign of just how badly off she was, she supposed.

"Sleep. You'll feel better next time you wake." He kept talking, but she was floating away now and couldn't make sense of the words.

The next time she woke, Trey was no longer there, only a normal. Familiar, as he was part of the team. Callie didn't trust him, didn't trust any nonshifters, even if this guy was innocuous enough.

She fed and drank and healed, and slept some more. It became her routine, a very basic existence and yet enough for the time being.

A week later the exhaustion was fading and her natural restlessness reasserted itself. She roamed the room, ready to move out, to move on—when Trey returned. The real Trey, this time. He gave her a once-over, and there was nothing sexual in it, never had been. She wished that absence didn't cause her a pang of regret.

"You're looking much better," he observed.

"Yes." The scars on her throat were vivid, but they no longer hurt. Unlike those of most of her past injuries, the scars wouldn't completely disappear. The feral had done too much damage and shifting couldn't erase them.

"Sit down, Callie."

She sighed, but complied. He liked to loom over people as he reamed them out.

He turned, and the intensity, the cold blaze of his blue eyes, took her aback, though she should have been familiar with his anger by now. "What the *fuck* did you think you were doing?"

"Debriefing," she drawled. "Is that what this is?"

He fisted a hand. "I could have sworn you didn't have a death wish, or I would never have sent you out there."

"You need me."

"Not like that I don't."

She opened her mouth to argue, then closed it again.

Briefly he shut his eyes. "I thought you were honest. I thought I could read you better than that."

"I *am* honest," she protested, piqued that the one person in the world she trusted thought otherwise. "I don't have a death wish." At his raised eyebrows, she pulled in a fortifying breath and tried to explain. "It's only..." They didn't talk like this, she and Trey, so finding the words was difficult. "When I meet a werecougar, that moment before leading them to their death, I always wish, just a little, that it was the last time. I don't actually want to be dead. I just don't want—" She broke off as she realized she'd been going to say, *I just don't want to kill any more of my kind.*

Was that true? Did she want to stop working for Trey?

Trey was the only person she had. And these cougars she lured in, they were death machines. They needed to be killed. For a shifter, killing was kinder than imprisonment. She knew all that, and yet had to revisit the rationale behind her job over and over again.

Trey's icy eyes bored into hers. "If it makes you feel any better, you're fired. You won't be bringing in another cougar. You've proved you can't."

The job was over. Stunned relief hit her, an almost physical force that winded her, and she leaned forward, taking in the news. But there was also loss. Trey had given her a home, a purpose, even a love, one-sided as it had been. Yet it wasn't in her to argue to stay. Her pride and his aloofness made it impossible. Instead she admitted, "I always thought we'd track down a puma who didn't need to be destroyed, who could be saved."

He shifted his head and shoulder, not quite a shrug. "That was my hope too."

"You've had much better luck with werewolves, eh?"

"Callie. These guys were probably on their own from the time they were toddlers. Werecougars, even more than werewolves, need to be raised by people, need to be socialized."

"Yeah." They'd already been through the differences between the pack dynamics of wolves and the solitary nature of cougars. The latter was fine in the real animal, but fucked up a shifter. She hated that conversation, even if Trey only spoke the truth.

"So, you thought this cougar could be saved?" he asked, gaze intent.

"He was young, Trey."

"Not young enough."

"You killed him, then." She'd known, but nevertheless Trey's nod hurt.

"I'd still like an explanation for what went wrong. Why you led him away, why you let him attack you."

So she spoke of the feral male's small size and young age and the way he'd chirped at her. To her embarrassment, her voice caught.

Looking unimpressed, Trey rolled right over that observation, that oh-so-brief connection that had meant so much to her. "You didn't have to let him rip your throat open because he *chirped*."

"Oh, that."

"Yeah that."

"I didn't think he would hurt me."

"He'd killed six people, including a small child, and he'd knocked you over. Yet you didn't think he would hurt you." Trey looked haunted now. Another first. She hadn't realized he felt so responsible for her well-being.

"He retracted his claws," she explained, though it sounded kind of stupid now.

Trey didn't speak, he waited for more. If he were in his wolf form, he'd look on full alert, ears forward, body tensed and ready for action.

"He swiped a paw down my belly."

"God, he could have eviscerated you too." He raked a hand through his too-short hair. "You wouldn't have recovered from both."

She nodded, inordinately warmed that he cared. Until now, until her almost-death, she hadn't known that she'd meant something to Trey. At least she could carry that knowledge with her after he kicked her off the base. That she was out of his life was obvious or he wouldn't be revealing this much emotion.

"He didn't gut me," she said, returning to that point. "His claws were retracted. So I thought he was playing. Until he tore my throat."

Trey actually winced.

"How did he die?" she asked.

"You mean, how did I save your life? I was wolf. When you didn't bring him into the clear as planned, I came after you. I attacked him. His throat, like yours, ripped open, but..." He threw up his hands. "You know these ferals. They're ignorant. He didn't know enough to shift immediately."

"Or didn't want to," she muttered.

"Possible," Trey allowed.

"He was too young. I wanted to help him."

"Unfortunately, he was already beyond helping."

Maybe, but Trey didn't really know. They would never

know. She didn't want to argue that point.

"When do I leave?" Whether he liked it or not, Trey had been her family these past four years. She would miss him. Her leave-taking would be painful.

He seemed rather taken aback by the abrupt question and his answer came out a bit gruff. "You have time to heal. There's no rush."

She fiddled with the hem of her shirt, the idea of being turned loose sinking in. "Maybe I'll go feral."

"Don't joke."

"Not a joke." She fixed her gaze on the blank wall in front of her. If he'd stayed her boss, she wouldn't have said it. However, her time here was over. "I don't know what to do with myself."

"Visit family."

At the suggestion, she almost snarled. She could feel her lip lift in a sneer. "You know I have next to none."

He shook his head, disagreeing with her. "Remember where I found you? Taking care of your foster sister, Ruth? You worry about her. You occasionally visit her. Go see how she's doing."

Chapter One

The smells were familiar—pine, cut grass and the heat of the earth rising. In this season, summer, she'd have to resort to shadows and night to accomplish anything. Like feeding. A necessity before the shift.

Her human self could not fend for itself. Puma's lip curled. She didn't entirely approve of her vulnerability in that bare, hairless skin. Yet she could not stay puma. After a time, the human pressed too hard upon her and she became lonely, starved of companionship.

The human, Callie, might call this home, but Puma was not yet ready to name it such. Twice before she'd been forced to flee from here, when cougar sightings had begun to alarm the residents. It would happen again and that thought was accompanied by a certain rather unfeline weariness.

Nevertheless, she had traveled far to reach what was undeniably familiar and comforting in its odd human way. In the safety of her cat body, she intended to inspect everything, to ensure, as much as was possible, a safe transition. She would also check on the sister for whom, even as Puma, she felt affection. Callie had half-raised the girl, given the neglect of her elderly foster mother.

Puma flicked her tail, feeling the long grass behind her bend with the motion, and approached the edge of the subdivision. Crouching, she surveyed the humans. Mostly children out and about, with bikes and scooters. One boy kicked a ball and chased after it, over and over again.

Her body tensed, her muscles bunched, though not with prey instinct, as the town had feared in the past and would fear again. She might have a cougar's form, and she might have a cougar's senses and some of its needs. But she wasn't a true feral and she was fond of human children, would have liked to care for one again, as she had for Ruth.

Pumas were solitary, but the females were meant to bear offspring and raise them. Impossible, however, to succeed in bearing offspring without a mate. The real cougars had nothing to do with her, nor she with them. Her human self, Callie, who *could* have mated, was not only stupidly skittish, but refused to conceive.

That memory made her tense. Human memory sat there, beneath the surface of her thoughts, muted by her puma, and not always easy to interpret. What Puma did understand was that the pressure to be human was building, and she could no longer ignore it. The cat disliked relinquishing control to her weaker half. From a survival point of view, it was unwise. However, other forces were at work and other needs. After years of fighting it, Puma had learned to submit to her human self. Otherwise she went crazy, lost control, found herself in strange situations, dangerous situations.

It would not be long now. If Puma was a solitary animal, the human was not and had begun to rage within. Callie had promised Trey she wouldn't go feral and her promise was half-broken, given that months had likely passed since she'd shifted and stalked away from the compound that had been home for four years. Trey didn't know just how hard her two halves warred, never quite able to find a healthy balance. One shouldn't be born to fight yourself, but somehow that was what

Puma and Callie had done, and continued to do.

Even her thoughts were turning human, in preparation for the shift. Puma did not usually analyze itself or its twin. She normally focused on more immediate needs.

Which now consisted of two short-term goals—to steal clothes off a line and locate the sister who had moved again. Her human self would find the new address.

Puma retreated through high grass and into the woods. It was several days, though, before she finally allowed herself to change.

Callie woke to panic, her mind a blur, her heart beating out of her chest, or so it felt. The disorientation immobilized her for long minutes until, with great strength of will, she shoved herself up to sitting and gulped air.

Where the fuck am I?

Sweat broke out all over her naked body. A warm breeze passed over her. Leaves shielded her from the sun above. Okay, it was summer, she was in some kind of copse, protected, but how—?

She sagged slightly as the realization crashed down on her. *Again.* She had just shifted from her cat body. *Puma*, something deep inside her insisted and Callie sighed, the noise a shaky release of air. The cat in her—*the puma* as Callie thought of it, though that wasn't a very healthy way to refer to one's self—had ideas of its own about how it should be referred to. Callie wondered if Puma disliked Callie quite as much as Callie disliked Puma.

Probably.

She wiped the sweat off her face and glanced around. Shivering, not from cold or hunger, but from the fear that always accompanied her reentry into the human world.

What had Puma done this time to prepare?

It now had the sense to find her clothes to wear. Otherwise she was a tad more visible than seemed wise. Puma had learned that the hard way, after the incident—"Police find naked, confused woman"—and she'd become Jane Doe and been hospitalized, making the puma in her wild with anger at such restrictions. Callie had barely gotten out of there alive. Ever since, the cat ensured Callie had clothing so she didn't need to explain her nudity or her temporary memory loss.

Callie dressed. No bra or underwear, but at least the gray shorts had a drawstring and didn't fall down. The T-shirt was overlarge, pink. Puma appeared to be drawn to pink clothes, if its past selections were any indication.

Pretty in pink.

She shook her head, not knowing where that phrase came from, and pressed a hand to her chest. The memories, her jumble of human memories, sometimes got lost in the shift and it took a few hours or days to disentangle them from the overly visual and largely meaningless catlike thoughts.

It all depended on how long Callie had been out. Neither she nor Puma liked to abdicate their form and though Callie knew enough that she could sense how wrong this internal war was, she couldn't figure out how to stop it. It was difficult to make links between the two of them. Occasionally she'd thought of confessing her private struggle to Trey, but had feared he would fire her. Well, she'd been fired and she still hadn't had the guts to spill. He hadn't known that once she left him the puma would resist shifting back to human without another shifter to encourage her to do so. Trey's human presence had always lured the puma back to Callie. Trey was the only shifter Callie had ever met, and no one else called to her. Except maybe Ruth.

Enough brooding on her split personality and her infatuation with her ex-boss. Today she remembered that Puma liked pink. Perhaps Callie's endless monologues about the dangers of staying cat too long had reached her other self. At least this time she hadn't been cat for years. That long stretch of cat life had happened in her early twenties and she had barely managed to stay in one piece.

She tugged at her hair. Callie tried to hack it off before shifting and use it as a marker of time when she returned to her human self, but didn't always succeed. Had she shorn her head before the last shift? She couldn't remember. Patience. She'd get hold of a calendar sooner rather than later, then she'd know the date.

For now the summer season and shoulder-length hair—she couldn't have been cat for more than half a year—were sufficient markers of the passage of time.

Callie wasn't hungry. A relief that the puma had known to fill her belly before the transition. Still, Callie was tired; shifting ate energy. So she curled up in the copse and slept, hoping the human dreams would jog all those memories she needed to cope with her human world.

She hoped, as she always hoped, to stay awhile.

Dev Malik ran behind the bicycle, hand on that plastic seat, while Madison wobbled her way along the bike path.

The little girl braked abruptly and Dev managed to stop

without tripping over his own feet, or the bike itself.

She turned around, accusation in her eyes. "You let go."

"Nope." He tilted his head towards his hand, still attached to the seat, and she followed his gaze.

The frown lightened, a lip got chewed.

"Want to try again?" he offered.

She gave one decisive nod. Dev gripped the handlebars, allowing her to get balanced, then pushed off, all the while holding that seat. He thought if he ever did remove his hand, Madison would never trust him again. She needed to trust someone in this topsy-turvy world she lived in. Inwardly, he sneered at himself. "Topsy-turvy" sounded benign, almost gently chaotic. Then again Dev's mind, such as it was, liked to shy away from thinking about how seriously fucked they all were.

He derailed that train of thought by giving his head a good shake, and continued running, hand attached to bike. Was it good or bad that Madison could do this for an hour straight? He wasn't sure there was any actual improvement in her balance, but the bigger point, that Madison enjoyed the activity, was what counted.

When his back began to complain and she began to tire, they made for home. He brought out popsicles and they sat on the porch in not-quite-companionable silence. He wasn't particularly good at small talk to start with and small talk with a seven-year-old baffled him enough to leave him tongue-tied. Even if they'd known each other for months. He thought. His concept of time was a little problematic these days given that he couldn't seem to track it.

At least her small face didn't have that pinched, worried expression it sometimes carried.

"I like orange," she declared.

He had to think for a moment to realize she referred to the popsicles and not the color in general.

"But I like grape too."

"Good." He smiled, she smiled back, and then that new young woman came out their front door.

Madison's face brightened. She stood and waved from two feet away. "Hi, Ruth!"

It came out more like *Wooth*. Incredibly cute, but Dev was a little alarmed that Madison even knew the woman's name. He hadn't remembered. Again. He hated these lacunae of memory.

"Hello...Ruth?" he ventured.

She stood there, jingling keys in her hand. Pretty, too much makeup, clothes just this side of skimpy, which Dev could appreciate in an abstract way. She wasn't quite his type and she was Scott's latest discovery. How long had she been here?

Dev found himself rubbing his eyes.

"You okay?" she asked.

"Oh yeah." He wasn't sure if he sounded sarcastic or sincere, but it didn't matter, they were the right words to say.

Ruth smiled, brilliantly. It didn't quite reach her eyes.

Dev jabbed an elbow out to indicate his companion. "Madison likes to bicycle."

"Good for you." Ruth winked at Madison who ducked her head.

"I'm Dev." He stuck out his hand and they shook. They should have been introduced, but it never worked that way. Or maybe, going by her puzzled expression, she knew he was Dev. "I guess you're staying with us for a while."

"I have been." She added, "Thanks for taking me in. Scott said you wouldn't mind."

"I don't mind." Dev didn't. He didn't at all.

She nodded, then fidgeted.

Dev could take a hint. "I'll let you go." With that Ruth jogged down the stairs to his car and drove away.

She crawled through the tall grass, made taller by the fact it was the human who crawled. Annoyance rippled through her. Why act like a cat when she was human? Puma flicked an invisible tail in irritation, as if whispering *safer*, and she continued on all fours. The night was still dry, the temperature not having dropped yet, and the light rustle of the wind calmed her.

She might act like a cat, but the memories were returning and would serve to acclimate her to her new form, Callie, who had a sister, Ruth. A baby sister, who was lost yet again—that email Callie had read today at the local library had her seriously alarmed. It was weeks old. Puma's fault, this delay, although one thing she knew was that the protective instinct stayed strong on both sides of the divide, cat or Callie. Ruth was hers to protect, even when or especially when her little sister was drawn to men who used their fists.

There was a new man. Ruth had named him Scott, had given this address where she lived.

Callie hissed. The puma wanted Ruth safe too, but the puma had little idea of time. Callie worried because her sister had never asked for help before. Any intervention had been at Callie's initiative, such as when she'd taken leave from Trey and come to kick out the last jerk to use Ruth as a punching bag.

Now Ruth had moved into a house she certainly could not

afford. *He has money,* Ruth had written from her gmail account to Callie's. It was such an odd note. *He bought me a computer. I love him, but he makes me nervous. Callie, can you come?*

A beam shone, passing over her, and Callie froze before sinking to the ground while coming full awake. To her horror she realized she'd been in some kind of trance, sleep...prowling. *Fuck.* She hated the first day after the shift. She acted stupid.

Yeah, Puma replied, though *she* had been the one not able to let go.

Callie lay flat on her stomach, her heart pounding. So Ruth's men problems were pathological, but what would you call Callie's problems? Bizarre? Psycho? Certainly untreatable.

"Hello?" A male voice, deepish, gravelly with sleep. God, had she been making cat noises? Callie loathed the way she was so out of control so much of the time. Well, that had been the bane of her existence—lack of control. It had moved her from foster home to foster home until some weary old woman who was wiser or lazier or more senile than the rest had refused to try to control Callie, letting her come and go as she wished.

Ruth had been the granddaughter of that woman, Sheena, and Sheena had been Ruth's guardian, as well as Callie's.

"Someone there?" The stranger persisted, his voice a little sharper. Callie breathed as quietly as possible, reminding herself that human hearing was inadequate.

Unfortunately, human feet didn't know this and they kept moving in her direction. He stopped in front of her and she desperately hoped, given the new moon, that he wouldn't see her.

A flashlight shone down on the back of her head.

Chapter Two

Callie chose to play dead, or at least act unconscious.

"Crap," he muttered, and in one swift motion was kneeling beside her. Deftly, he found her pulse and exhaled relief as his warm, blunt fingers pressed into her neck. Personally, Callie thought her pulse was too fast and shallow, but if he'd thought she were dead, no doubt any pulse would do.

He turned her over and the sensation of being touched flowed through her body in a wave she couldn't suppress. She had thought she would flinch and stiffen at this unusual contact. Instead, it was surprisingly easy to lie loose and accept his hands on her, hands that were respectful, careful. She liked his smell too. Clean, hint of perspiration on this balmy night.

He shone the light on her face and it was all she could do not to squint. As he shifted again, she sensed...fear? Yes, his heart rate was speeding up. How odd. She didn't think she was very frightening in this form, but something had unnerved him. Her face? She tried to remember her face in greater detail—it was unremarkable, she was sure. Perhaps the scars on her neck were disturbing to the eye? She'd forgotten about them till now, but they should have faded to white lines where they'd be noticeable in daylight, but hard to discern at night.

"Hey." He rocked her, not very hard. Like a nudge to rouse her. "Shit," he exhaled, then pulled in a long, rough breath.

She heard high-pitched electronic beeps, a number of them, and despite her stupidity and temporary amnesia, she recognized what was going on. This had happened before, someone calling in as if she was an emergency. She could *not* be Jane Doe again. Not in this place.

She jackknifed to sitting and hit his wrist, knocking the phone out of his hand. He let out a *whoof* of surprise as he fell backwards and went silent, still. The flashlight dropped to the grass, its light muted.

"No ambulance." She reached over and picked up the phone, turned it off. Though the night was moonless, her eyesight, courtesy of Puma, was excellent. His brown eyes met hers. They were still dilating, getting used to the dark without the flashlight's bright beam. His gaze was slightly unfocused as he tried to make out her features in the night.

"What, exactly, are you doing here?" He sounded relieved and a little confused, not accusing. Callie supposed that he'd been worried something was seriously wrong with her.

"Uh, I got lost," she said lamely, her voice hoarse from disuse. She rubbed her throat as if that would help her along when it came to speech.

As he pushed himself back up to crouching, the phone-wielding man's expression became wry. "Okay if I take back my cell?" He held out a hand and she dropped it in his palm.

"Just don't call anyone," she warned.

"Ever?"

"About me."

He frowned.

"I mean..." God, she needed to sound halfway normal here or she could get in trouble. "I mean, there is no need to worry about me and call the police. I'm fine and I won't..." Okay, *attack you* was not the right way to finish this sentence, so she settled on, "I mean you no harm."

One eyebrow went high in question, or perhaps disbelief. That was good. He didn't perceive her to be a threat. She glanced down at herself and hoped she looked unprepossessing in an oversized pink T-shirt and ragged gray shorts.

He pushed up to standing. Following his lead, she rolled to her feet to face him and brushed off her backside while he watched. She didn't mind this scrutiny, which was odd, given her habitual dislike of normals. Whether he smelled good or not, she should stay on her guard. Instead, she wanted to make friends. She could practically hear her puma hissing, *stupid human.*

"You still haven't answered my first question," he pointed out. She cast her mind back, trying to remember the question. "Why are you here?"

"Oh right. Sorry." Time to bite the bullet, though she was going to be really disappointed if this guy was the Scott who made her sister nervous. Callie's first impression was that of a nice guy, but Ruth didn't get involved with nice guys and Callie's first impressions were not always accurate. "I'm looking for Ruth Langer."

"Ruth?" He stiffened and his face went blank. Tension wafted off him and the return of his fear had Callie scratching her head. She'd expected him to ridicule her for crawling around in the grass, not freeze up at the mention of her sister's name. "You're looking for Ruth in my backyard?"

"*Your* backyard? Are you Scott then?"

"No." To Callie's relief, his denial was swift and...angry. Maybe he didn't like Scott either.

"I thought Ruth lived here." When he didn't answer, Callie added, "175 Woodbury Avenue, right?"

He opened his mouth. Closed it again. Clearly disturbed, he also seemed to be struggling to remember something, and failing. "This is my house, yes."

You sure? Callie wanted to ask, given how confused he suddenly seemed, but she decided to stick to questions about her sister. "And is Ruth here?"

He just gazed at her darkly.

"Hello?" tried Callie when he didn't answer.

Still no response. Though she could swear he was perfectly aware of her, he didn't move for close to minute. At a loss, Callie waited and then, for wont of something better to do in this new-to-her situation, she clapped her hands in front of his face. The sharp noise echoed in the night. The man blinked, but otherwise didn't react, didn't seem to focus. Callie felt distinctly uneasy.

Okay, well, Nice But Odd Guy would just have to wait. The search for Ruth came first.

"I'll take that as a yes." She ducked around him, determined to get to her sister. Maybe this *was* the Scott who made Ruth nervous. He was certainly beginning to make Callie nervous.

"Hey," he protested.

From behind her, Callie felt movement and with ease she evaded the man's grasp, broke into a run and leapt up the steps. Three long strides and she flung the door open.

She'd meant to call out for her sister, but as she entered the house, she was brought up short by a little girl in a nightdress. The blonde child stood in a hall leading to the kitchen. It occurred to Callie that dashing into a stranger's home was perhaps not her most-well-thought-out action ever, but she'd been worried about Ruth after Dark Eyes had gone into a trance.

31

She heard him shut the door. The little girl's blue gaze moved from Callie to the man behind her. Relief showed on her small face and her shoulders relaxed. Callie felt bad that she had scared the young.

"Dev?" The girl tried to edge towards this Dev while keeping a good distance from the strange woman who'd barged into her home.

Callie turned and backed up, allowing the child to get by her.

"Hey, Madison, you should be sleeping." His voice was calm, reassuring, but his body language was not. His lean body—near Callie's height, perhaps a little taller—screamed tension, and his fist was clenched before he unfurled it to place a hand on Madison's head and stroke a mess of blonde hair.

Madison jammed a thumb in her mouth and curled an arm around Dev's leg. After a few moments of silence, while Callie debated the merits of asking after Ruth again, Madison pulled out her thumb and fixed her gaze on Callie. "Who are you?"

"My name's Callie." She paused, then added hopefully, "Ruth's sister?"

Madison's face lit up while Dev's just darkened.

"I like Ruth," the girl declared.

"So do I." Callie heard footsteps above her, tentative but definitely belonging to a human. "Ruth?" she shouted.

"Omygod!" came back with that familiar squeal, and relief flooded Callie. Ruth was alive and moving, given that Callie now heard feet thundering down the stairs. She strode through the hall as Ruth reached the landing and, without stopping, launched herself into Callie's arms. Under the force of Ruth's airborne embrace, Callie staggered back. Her shoulders hit the wall. The contact shook Callie, not just physically, but emotionally. It had been more than a year since she'd last seen

Ruth, and during that time no one else had done much more than shake Callie's hand.

She shuddered in a breath and another, to fight the sensation of being overwhelmed, then locked her legs, to make sure her knees didn't buckle as she leaned back against the wall.

"I'm so glad to see you," Ruth declared fiercely, her voice low.

Ruth had never been quite this intense in her greeting, although the absence of joy also puzzled Callie. Usually Ruth would disengage and begin jumping around, but she clung until Callie set Ruth down to inspect her. Making sure she was in one piece, Callie touched her sister's head and face, checking for bruises until Ruth batted her hands away impatiently.

"Stop that, I'm fine. I'm just glad to see you," Ruth added, at Callie's frown.

Callie released a long, shaky breath. Ruth was safe. In fact, she looked healthier than usual, as if she might be eating properly, which was not exactly Ruth's habit. She also didn't smell of nicotine. Weird. Callie was hard-pressed to imagine her sister had quit smoking.

Ruth stared up at her with shining eyes. "Now you can fix everything."

"*Fix* everything?" Generally, Callie beat up the latest bully that Ruth called a boyfriend and moved Ruth to a safer locale. "You mean…Scott?"

"Callie has to go. *Immediately.*" The voice seemed to come out of nowhere and Callie almost jumped at the intrusion. She'd been so preoccupied by this reunion that she'd completely forgotten about Dev whose persona had undergone a rather rapid change in the short time she'd been acquainted with him. Right now his commanding tone brooked no argument and

Callie was irritated. Did he think that being male gave him some kind of authority over her? Wrong. Trey's authority had been earned and Callie doubted she'd ever admire anyone again.

"Excuse me?" asked Callie in, she thought, an intimidating manner. When she injected some anger into her voice, humans often reacted with unease. As if they sensed she wasn't quite one of them.

But Dev ignored Callie and stared at Ruth, a rather haggard air to him now. His dark eyes were mesmerizing, an observation that somehow surprised her, even made her feel rather warm despite the circumstances. Ruth, however, didn't appear much affected by Dev or his eyes.

Instead, she placed an arm around Callie's waist and, like a twelve-year-old, tossed her head at him. "My big sister stays with me."

Madison had followed Dev down the hall and reached up to pull at his shirt, thumb again in mouth, so Dev bent to pick her up.

"Why would I have to go?" For the child's sake, Callie made it a point to sound conversational, not confrontational. At first impression, Dev had seemed reasonable. Surely that couldn't be a complete illusion.

Despite her question, Callie didn't actually plan to stay here long. Taking off was her usual modus operandi when she rescued Ruth. However, Dev's reaction to Callie's appearance made her curious.

Dev's gaze never left Ruth. He didn't acknowledge Callie's question. A little rude. Callie was a person too. Okay, she was shifter, but Dev sure as heck didn't know that.

"It's not safe for your sister to stay," he told Ruth. He gazed at her as if his eyes were sending a coded message to Ruth who would understand. Underneath the flat words was a kind of...entreaty?

Ruth evidently refused to understand. "Callie can look after herself. She's *strong.*"

Dev jerked his head, an impatient gesture. "Can I speak to you in private, Ruth?" Although phrased as a question, it was still a demand.

Ruth dug in her heels, and Callie sensed uncertainty behind the stubbornness. "No. I don't hide anything from my sister."

"You don't, eh?" His lips twisted. Cynicism overlay his tension. "God help me, that's rich."

Beside her, Ruth stared right back at Dev, expression belligerent, but she did begin biting her nails.

"What do you mean by that?" Callie asked Dev. She'd started out liking the guy, because he'd wanted to help her when he'd thought she was hurt. Then she'd softened when Madison had turned to him for comfort and safety. Callie had even been relieved he wasn't Scott. But now? Well his attitude sucked. She needed to get Ruth out of here.

Dev again had this air of looking for what he wanted to say and being unable to find the words. It went on for some time and Callie stood there impatiently while Ruth seemed to find the silence normal, if not boring. Finally Dev swallowed and his shoulders bowed. Callie thought the look of defeat was overly melodramatic.

He turned his gaze on her, the first time during this exchange. "I've never even heard that Ruth had a sister." His suspicious tone suggested that Ruth had deliberately hidden a crucial fact.

Callie expected Ruth to qualify their relationship and explain about their being foster sisters, but she just drew closer to Callie, nestling into her shoulder.

"I kept it private." Ruth looked up, her expression pleading, as if she'd offered Callie a great insult. "That's why, Callie. Privacy."

"Don't worry about it," she said automatically, though she didn't remember Ruth ever valuing privacy before. Found it a bit odd, truth be told. Then again, why should Ruth talk to this jerk about Callie? Wasn't that the bigger issue?

Okay, the entire conversation was weird. She thought. Maybe Callie wasn't used to human conversation, being cat too often. Even taking that into account, everything felt off. Ruth's pleading. Dev's silences. He might be some kind of control freak. Though Callie frowned slightly as Madison burrowed into him, eyelids drooping while Dev absentmindedly gave her a pat on the back. An affectionate control freak prone to trances?

Squeezing Ruth's shoulders, Callie said, "Let's sleep on it. We can talk in the morning."

"I'm putting Madison back to bed," Dev growled at Ruth and stalked by them and up the stairs.

Once Dev was out of sight, Callie whispered, "*What* is his problem? He seems kind of erratic. Ruth, why are you living with him?"

No longer meeting Callie's gaze, Ruth actually shuffled her feet, and Callie was reminded of that period of time when Ruth used to sneak out to buy crystal meth with her friends. Callie could almost hear the alarm bells ringing in her head, spurred on by her sister's suddenly shifty behavior. *Fuck.*

"What is it, Ruth?" Callie kept her voice low, even.

"Dev's okay." Ruth shrugged. "It's his house, after all."

"So...you're with him?" They hadn't acted like lovers that Callie could tell, but she was no expert.

"No, I'm Scott's."

Callie didn't much like that description.

"Dev just helps out," Ruth added as if that completely clarified their relationship. "He likes helping people."

"Uh, 'helps out'? What does that *mean*?"

"It means he's helpful."

"You're being evasive, Ruth. What's going on?"

"You're here." Ruth looked up, her smile brilliant again, a little too forced and yet there was meaning behind it. "I'm *so* glad to see you."

Okay, questions weren't getting answered. Callie decided to give up on them. Time to focus on action. "We have to get you out of here."

Ruth immediately shook her head. "I can't leave."

"You can't leave," Callie repeated slowly, trying to make sense of this.

"No."

"Because...?"

Ruth licked her lips. "I stay here."

"Because...?"

Ruth's gaze darted left, right, even down.

"Help me out here, Ruth. Come on." She paused. Waiting. "Give me something to work with. Because you're not making a lot of sense." While Callie still hoped that maybe her limited human interaction was clouding her judgment and everything was just peachy, Ruth's demeanor suggested no such thing.

"Don't ask, okay, Callie?" That pleading again, this time in her voice since her face was hidden.

Callie felt tired. It was late and Ruth's behavior was freaking her out. No doubt Callie was reacting to the shift back into human society. She needed some time to adjust to people. The only person she'd spent much time with lately had been Trey, a closemouthed werewolf, who could hardly prepare her for normal human interaction. "Why don't we sleep on it?"

"That's a *great* idea."

"It is?" Hardly a genius idea, despite Ruth's oddball enthusiasm.

Ruth was already walking up the stairs, looking back to beckon Callie forward. As Callie caught up, Ruth spoke again. "I don't care what Dev thinks. I'm glad you're here. You're strong."

"Uh-huh." Callie couldn't remember Ruth ever praising her strength before. She hoped Ruth made more sense in the morning.

Chapter Three

Callie woke as soon as feet hit the floor—Dev's, she assumed. The footsteps were too heavy to be Madison's, and Ruth still slept beside her on this queen-sized bed.

They hadn't talked more last night. A year apart, and Ruth had definitely changed. She didn't want to talk. Well, beyond declaring an uncomfortable number of times that she was *very* glad Callie was here.

Callie needed to think. Observe and think, because, yeah, she was *so* insightful when it came to people. She ground her teeth—quietly—and wished she had more human experience to draw upon in order to figure out what was going on. The situation was new and didn't resemble any of Ruth's past living arrangements.

Ruth seemed nervous, her words and actions forced, including throwing herself into Callie's arms. Had that display been for Dev? God knows, Ruth had an unnerving tendency to try to be whoever her current boyfriend wanted her to be, though doting sister was not usually a quality her men looked for.

And Dev didn't fit the mold of men Ruth was drawn to. Okay, maybe he brooded and hinted at dire consequences, but there'd been no violence simmering beneath the surface, ready to let loose. When he'd gotten fed up with Ruth, he went and put a little girl to bed.

So perhaps the absent Scott fit the mold. Except he wasn't even here.

Opening her eyes, Callie looked at the stippled ceiling and gave up on piecing together the puzzle of Ruth. Time to convince her sister to leave, and if that somehow didn't work, Callie would meet Scott and see how he fit into this household.

Callie lay still and listened while Dev made Madison pancakes—goodness, what an attentive soul he was—and Madison whined about the orange juice. Then the low background noise of a TV began.

A while later Ruth slid out of bed, and Callie allowed her to think she still slept, curious as to what Ruth would do next. It was nothing surprising. She got dressed and stumbled downstairs to make coffee and talk to Dev. Callie's hearing was exceptional, but she couldn't understand Dev's low-level muttering with the TV on. All she could decipher was Ruth's repeated "we're not supposed to talk" until Dev raised his voice to declare he was *not* talking.

Huh?

Then he slammed out of the house and Callie decided now was as good a time as any to get out of bed.

She made her way down and found Ruth in the kitchen munching on a pancake. Ruth pointed a fork to a plate of them. "Dig in."

"He made enough breakfast for us all?" asked Callie.

"Of course." The question surprised Ruth. "Dev always cooks."

"Of course."

Unaware of the sarcasm, Ruth slid out of the kitchen and into the den. Callie followed to observe from the doorway that

Madison was sucking on her thumb and watching a commercial for McDonald's.

"It's ten o'clock," Ruth announced. "Time for *Sesame Street*. You remember *Sesame Street*, don't you, Callie?"

"Ah yes," she answered slowly. She nibbled her pancake, savoring the human food after months of doing without. It was quite good, though Callie was not a fussy eater. Gazing out the window, she saw a well-groomed backyard and beyond that the woods from which she had come last night.

"Callie," called Ruth.

Callie walked away from the view and over to her sister. "What?"

Ruth patted the cushion beside her, as if Callie should be excited by Big Bird's entry onto the screen. "Sit with me."

"I don't like watching TV, remember?" It made her restless.

"Oh." Ruth shrugged, but before she could focus on the TV again, Callie tugged on Ruth's arm, pulling her up from the couch. Reluctantly, her little sister followed Callie out of the room.

"What?" Ruth demanded, apparently annoyed to be missing Big Bird's morning debut.

"I think," Callie began, "we'd better talk, especially since Dev is out."

This suggestion caused Ruth some alarm for she stepped back, her gaze sliding away. "Dev will return soon. He always does."

"Okay." Callie bit her lip. She felt somewhat at sea. "Just tell me, what is the scoop on you and Dev? Why are you living in his house?"

Ruth cast about for an answer, acting baffled by the question. Callie was eerily reminded of Dev last night when he hadn't answered simple questions. "Ruth?" she said softly.

"I thought you didn't like to chat." At least Ruth wasn't going into a trance like Dev seemed to, but it wasn't much of an answer.

"Sometimes I do."

"Since when?"

"Since now, when my little sister started acting so weird."

"You're not even my real sister."

Callie rubbed her forehead. "Then why'd you email me for help?"

"I didn't." Ruth lifted a shoulder, aiming for a casual gesture, but the attempt was marred by those darting eyes. Callie couldn't remember Ruth darting her eyes around before. It disturbed her.

"So you don't want me here?" Callie didn't know if she was hurt or pissed, but before she could decide Ruth threw arms around Callie's neck and fervently declared, "*Of course*, I want you here. I *love* you." Ruth never said she loved anyone. "I want you here but just don't talk so much, okay?" She pulled Callie closer, causing her neck to bend uncomfortably. "You know?"

"I do not know." Callie didn't keep the irritation out of her voice, and Ruth let go, backing up, face wary, a little defiant. Callie reached out to stop her. "You don't like *Sesame Street*, for God's sakes."

"I do too."

"Ruth, now you're scaring me."

Ruth's voice lowered to a whisper. "It's just better to keep quiet." She cast a furtive glance at the door.

"Are you scared of Dev?"

"Dev?" Ruth looked incredulous. "How could I be scared of Dev?"

42

"You tell me."

"Don't be silly, Callie. He's like me. He's fine. He cooks."

Okay.

Madison appeared in the doorway, big blue eyes gazing up at Callie. "I'm not scared of Dev. Ruth isn't either. Because Dev's our friend. He looks after us."

Callie pulled in a breath, not really wanting the child to enter into this bizarre conversation. She just nodded, to acknowledge what Madison had said. Then tried to shift the topic. "How old are you, Madison?"

"Seven. How old are you?"

Callie had to think for a moment.

Ruth rolled her eyes. "Twenty-eight, Callie. Why do you never remember your age?" She turned to Madison. "Eight years older than me and she sometimes thinks she's my mother." Ruth's laugh sounded a bit hollow.

Into the awkward silence that followed, Madison asked Callie, "Are you my friend?"

Callie, after a brief pause, decided to say "Yes."

Madison gave her a sweet smile. "Are you Scott's?"

"Don't ask that," Ruth snapped and Madison cringed.

"Ruth," chided Callie. Her sister could have a little more patience for the child who was actually quite charming.

Ruth glared. "I'm going out." She flounced off, up the stairs, and Callie was left with Madison and her question. Callie cocked her head. "No, I'm not Scott's friend."

"You belong to Scott?"

Recalling how last night Ruth had declared herself "Scott's", Callie winced. "No." An emphatic *no.* She found herself choking out the question, "Do you?" She was getting an awful, creepy feeling about the absent Scott.

Madison slowly nodded. "It's okay though. He's not a bad one. Even if he tells you not to talk. That's why Ruth tries not to. But it's hard for her."

What the hell? Callie couldn't really understand what Madison meant, though it didn't sound good, so she chose her next words carefully. Seven years old or not, Madison might be her best source of information. "So Scott told you not to talk?"

"Not me. I never talk in front of him. He thinks I don't speak." Madison's blue eyes grew bigger, as if she was in danger. "Don't let Scott know I can, okay?"

"Okay," Callie agreed. "Why is it a secret?"

Madison looked upward while she chewed on her lip. Her expression indicated she was thinking hard about how to explain it all to Callie. "Scott would have to tell me what to do then, and Dev doesn't like that. It's not good for my brain when my brain is still growing. Unlike his."

"Uh...not good for your brain, how?" At the child's frustrated frown, Callie added, "If it isn't good for you, I'll certainly keep your secret from Scott."

Madison nodded, pleased at that, and Callie decided she had a few choice words for Scott for casting this shadow over Madison, even if it was a shadow that Callie could not yet make sense of.

"Dev told me to never talk in front of Scott and then I'd be safer, and Dev's smart. Smarter than most of Scott's."

Callie felt a sick, sinking sensation in her stomach. Absent or not, Scott appeared to be a controlling person. "Who else is Scott's?"

Madison licked her lips and acquired that expression Dev and Ruth had when they clearly didn't want to say anything.

"Never mind," Callie said quickly, unwilling to put this little girl in a trance. "Maybe, when Scott visits, I won't talk either."

At that, Madison looked sad. "Dev says that only works with children."

"Ah. He might have a point. Only, what's wrong with talking?"

Madison shrugged her shoulders dramatically, a big rise and fall. "Scott doesn't like it."

Huh. Well, Scott, whether he liked it or not, was going to get an earful from Callie.

"Scott doesn't sound like the best type of friend." Callie racked her brain for an appropriate but neutral question for the child, something unrelated to Scott and talking. "So, who else is your friend? Besides Dev." Kind of lame, but hopefully not trance-inducing.

Madison blinked, then smiled. "Hannah."

"Does she live on your street?"

Madison snorted as if Callie had asked if the sky were green. "*No.* She lives in Malibu." At Callie's frown, Madison explained, "Hannah Montana. I don't have any real-life friends. Scott wouldn't like it."

With that, Madison turned around and walked back into the den, stuck her thumb back in her mouth and stared at the TV. Seven years old, thumb in mouth, no friends because *Scott wouldn't like it.* Callie didn't have a good feeling about this at all. Her maternal instincts were aroused, and now she wanted to take Ruth *and* Madison away from this weird house. From Scott.

Ruth came back down the stairs, now dressed, and wore a worried expression as she entered the kitchen. She clutched Callie's arm and Callie tried not to look fed up. "What now,

Ruth?"

"Don't be mad, okay?"

Callie sighed. "I'm trying."

Ruth seized on this like it was a great reprieve. "Oh good. It's just that we haven't seen each other for a while and you're a bit of a loner."

"What does that have to do with anything?"

Ruth ignored the question. "Listen, let's go out and..." She appeared to search for what they would do. Usually, Ruth wanted to go out for coffee and cake, but that would give them an opportunity to *talk*. So it was a no-go.

As Madison laughed at *Sesame Street*, Callie lifted her chin towards the child. "We can't leave a seven-year-old by herself."

Ruth flapped her hand towards the den. "It's all right."

"Ruth," said Callie, frowning.

"We can wait until Dev's finished running if you want."

"You don't care?" Callie didn't hide her disapproval.

"Madison never does anything." This statement appeared to explain everything, but at Callie's gaping mouth, Ruth dropped her voice and added, "She doesn't talk properly, you see. Scott says she's autistic."

Autistic, my ass, but something warned Callie not to dispute this with her sister. "All the more reason to stay until Dev is back."

Ruth smiled. "Okay! See we can agree on things."

Callie squinted a little as she asked her next question. "When do I get to meet Scott?" She expected Ruth to, at best, fob off the question, or perhaps throw a fit.

Instead, Ruth's face brightened even further. "That's a *great* idea, Callie."

Hmmm, Callie's second great idea in as many days.

"Besides, I *should* tell him when there's anyone hanging around the house, even if I do know them. Right?" Ruth picked up the phone off its cradle and walked away.

"Right," murmured Callie. *Hanging around?* She'd thought she was *visiting,* but whatever the case she was going to eavesdrop on this telephone conversation of Ruth and Scott's.

As she moved to follow her sister, Dev walked through the front door, dripping sweat and looking like he carried the weight of the world on his shoulders.

He'd kept his head clear during the run. Mostly by closely observing everything around him. The leaves, the squirrels, the small lake he passed by. The asphalt path he ran along. The blue jay.

When that hadn't been enough to distract him, he had mentally chanted: *don't think, don't think, don't think.*

He was turning into a blithering idiot.

The newest woman, Callie, was staring at him and he couldn't even bring himself to look at her. Instead, he wiped the sweat from his face with his T-shirt.

"Good run?" she asked.

Answerable. "Yes."

"Thanks for the pancakes."

He met her gaze then, blinking as he waded through the mass of obstacles that made up his brain and found this morning's activities—he'd made everyone pancakes.

"I'm the cook." He tried for a smile, but probably didn't make it past a grimace.

"You like to cook?"

Answerable. "Yes, thanks."

She was watching him too carefully. "Thanks?"

God, sometimes Ruth was perfectly right. *Don't talk.*

"I need a shower. Ciao."

"Dev?" Callie's voice stopped him halfway to the stairs. He should have ignored her, but it was hard. He was so damned *hungry* for someone new.

"Can Madison speak?"

Cold panic invaded. He should have told the child not to talk this morning, prevented it last night. It would help if he could keep his brain straight. "No," he managed, trying not to choke on his denial.

"Is she...?"

"Autistic." He grabbed that word, held on, because it protected Madison. *"Yes."*

Callie gazed at him, eyes wide and warm and amber. Really a delightful color and in another life, he would have been quite taken by her. "I still like her, Dev." The words were cautious, but Callie didn't argue the point about autism. That was the important thing and he could breathe more easily knowing it.

"She's a good kid. Just..." He didn't know what to say. *Different?* God knows whoever came to this house was different, and not in a good way.

"Dev," said Callie quickly. "Who's Scott?"

Dev stiffened. Impossible to explain, and yet his mouth spoke the words as if they came naturally to him. "He's a good friend of mine." He walked backwards to the stairs, then suddenly turned and dashed up them. Mention of Scott always left him in a state of confusion, but Dev was alert enough to feel embarrassed by his strange behavior.

Instead of jumping into the safety of a long, cold, mind-numbing shower, he heard Ruth's voice.

Wrong.

She shouldn't be on the phone. Almost of its own volition, his hand wrenched the door to her room open. She immediately stood, one palm held up in surrender while her other hand gripped the phone. "It's okay, Dev. I'm only talking to Scott. *He's glad I phoned.*" Her arm shot out towards him, phone in hand, as she offered him proof. "He wants to talk to you."

Dev's gut twisted, but he took the phone. He didn't keep Scott waiting. After all, Scott was a busy man. When had Scott become a man? Last year? Dev could swear he'd been a boy... Fuck, brain, *shut up.*

"Dev? It's me." Scott sounded concerned, and not all that old. "Have you met this sister of Ruth's?"

Dev swallowed so he could speak through his dry throat. "Yes."

"Is she asking questions?"

"Yes."

Scott swore.

Dev broke out in a sweat again, but he had to try to protect this innocent woman who had stumbled upon them, who could still get away unharmed if only she'd leave immediately. So he prevaricated, though it hurt to go against the rules. "Not so very many questions, really, Scott. Not very interesting."

"Doesn't matter. Give the phone back to Ruth."

It took a moment for Dev to unclench his hand from the phone as Ruth retrieved it. She cast him a short look of commiseration, before she was back speaking to Scott with her usual animation.

Dev managed to find his way to the shower and ran cold water, staying there until his teeth chattered. It didn't do much to clear his mind, though.

Because his mind no longer belonged to him.

Chapter Four

It was time to read his notes. Dev hated doing it, hated the way it made him feel, but steeled himself for the task. Because he needed to know what was true and what was the illusion Scott had cast.

Dev dried off, wrapped a towel around his waist and walked out of the bathroom, almost running into Callie who seemed to appear out of nowhere.

Her gaze drifted down his chest before she lifted her face to look straight at him. There was something like admiration in that short assessment, and he should have been flattered that a beautiful woman admired him while he stood half-naked before her. Yet he observed it all from a distance, given that he had no sexual drive to speak of.

It wasn't in his nature.

"Are you okay?" asked Callie.

Dev realized he'd been staring, as if she was the answer to something, though what that answer could be, he didn't know.

"Of course I'm okay," he said brusquely. "Do you mind if I get dressed?"

The flush rose quickly to her cheeks, but he had no time for regret. If he didn't keep his mind on track, he was going to forget to read his notes. And the reason he had to read his notes was because she'd arrived unexpectedly in his house. Without Scott's approval. No one came here without Scott's approval. Only Callie didn't know the rules.

He shut the door firmly behind him. Wished she'd vanish into thin air. It struck him, as it should have before now, that the way she'd arrived was exceedingly strange, crawling around in the high grass behind his yard. He'd thought he'd heard a cat. He'd been sitting outside in the dark evening, enjoying the simple smells, the simple sounds, trying to get rid of the noise in his head. The outside noise, unusual, out of place, had alerted him.

Such an odd way to look for one's sister. Though not as odd as his life, or Ruth's life, or Madison's.

Notes, he reminded himself. He needed to stay on track or his brain wandered off to do its own thing, and he forgot what he wanted to accomplish. So, notes. He kept them in the false bottom of his desk drawer, though perhaps that wouldn't really fool Scott or his colleagues. Still, no one had dislodged the strategically placed scrap of paper from the last time he'd closed it.

He didn't think.

His fingers scrambled to push the mechanism up, and the drawer pulled out fully so he could reach his piece of paper at the back. Written to himself.

At the top, in block letters, underlined, as if he were a drooling idiot who wouldn't recognize that this was important—and perhaps that was exactly what he was, Dev thought grimly—he had written:

STAY AWAY FROM ELEANOR AND MAX

The names caused a shudder to course through Dev, but despite the frisson of horror associated with them, he couldn't actually remember who Eleanor and Max were.

Yes, the memory lapses made him sick. Move on.

He kept reading, relieved that the numbered sentences were easier to understand.

1. Scott rescues people, including you.

Dev winced, because it must be true and yet he couldn't remember being rescued. It made him feel dizzy, and with a sense of déjà vu, he wondered if he should just rip this paper up so he wouldn't have to read it again.

No.

2. It is not useful to hate Scott. He's not all bad. It could be WORSE.

It sounded like something he'd write, a long time ago, before he became bitter and twisted with hate. He shied away from thinking about what "worse" with its capital letters meant. He'd learned not to force his brain into dark corners. It accomplished nothing.

3. You love your family but you must not contact them.

Okay. He didn't much remember loving his family anyway. The idea of family just made him numb.

4. Helen arrived September 30. Left January 24.

A vague image of a redhead, face freckled, not young, not old. Gone.

5. Ian arrived November 28. Left March 20.

Another vague image. Brown hair, heavy build, sad eyes.

6. Madison arrived December 3. Madison must not speak.

This one was familiar, that last sentence even underlined. Dev breathed easier because he never forgot that in being autistic, Madison was not considered attention-worthy, and flew under Scott's radar. Dev frowned, wishing he could remember where Madison came from. Did her parents miss her?

7. Ruth arrived May 22.

Dev's heart rate kicked up. He could have sworn she'd only been here a week or so. Hadn't he just recently known her name? So he read it again, to make sure.

Damn, Scott was messing with him about Ruth's arrival. Why did Scott want him to believe Ruth had only recently moved in when it had been two months ago? Because—Dev checked his watch—it was July now.

Okay, okay, didn't matter. He tried to shut down the rage that accompanied the realization that Scott was pushing him. Again.

Instead, Dev picked up his pen and added number eight.

8. Callie, Ruth's sister, arrived July 11.

Dev hoped that he wouldn't be able to make sense of that sentence the next time he picked up this paper. He hoped for her sake that Callie would be gone.

Callie learned that Scott was driving down from another city, four hours away, to deal with the emergency that was Ruth's sister's arrival.

Not that Ruth put it that way. "He just wants to meet you," she declared, as if Callie were concerned about Scott's good opinion.

She was not. In fact, she was spoiling for a fight. She and Puma, and she had to admit it was rather nice to be in partnership about this. Puma did not like this Scott, even at this distance.

Despite her reaction, her desire to go toe-to-toe with Scott, a part of Callie wondered if it would be in Ruth's best interest to get away before Scott arrived. Violence did Ruth no good at all. The truth was, Callie didn't much like it. Wouldn't be good for Madison either. On the other hand, Callie felt uneasy about leaving Madison behind in this strange house. Even Dev didn't appear to be comfortable in his own home. Perhaps, he, too, wasn't safe. Puma wanted to rescue them all.

However, Callie had to float the option of leaving. Ruth was the one she was responsible for. Dev didn't seem to even like Callie.

"Maybe we should go." Seeing Ruth's blank face, Callie clarified, "You know, take off. *Leave.*" Callie put it forth in as casual a manner as possible.

It seemed like such a revolutionary idea that it still took a few moments for Ruth to understand what exactly Callie was proposing. When she did, a horrified "No!" was her sister's reaction. At the baffled expression on Callie's face, Ruth collected herself. "I mean, I really want you two to meet, Cal." She twisted her hands, staring down like answers lay in them. "You see, Scott is very special to me."

"Oh, I'm beginning to think he's special, all right. You've never had a boyfriend quite like this."

Ruth blushed, looking coy and *gratified.* Ugh. "Callie," she protested too hard. "Scott is not my boyfriend. We're just friends."

"Is he cute then?"

Her little sister blinked, like the question needed to be puzzled out.

"Ruth?"

"Looks don't always matter."

Since when? thought Callie. Looks had always mattered to

Ruth. If nothing else, her past boyfriends had been attractive.

"I like what's inside Scott," Ruth said quietly, uncharacteristically smug about it, and Callie wanted to shake her.

They were in the kitchen, Ruth drinking water, Callie searching for some juice in the overcrowded fridge. "My God, you guys aren't going to go hungry with all this food." The fridge was packed full.

Ruth smiled vacantly.

"Should we make dinner tonight?" Callie wasn't particularly good at cooking, but she liked working in the kitchen. There was a novelty in dealing with human food, and she would appreciate being kept busy by something while waiting for "special" Scott.

"No." Ruth dismissed the idea. "Dev cooks."

"I have noticed he cooks. Does that mean no one else can?"

"Dev cooks," Ruth repeated in that newly disturbing way of hers. "Not me." At Callie's expression, she added, "That's what Scott likes."

"Uh-huh. Well, I happen to think that *Scott* will like *me* to cook." Callie started pulling out vegetables for a salad. Salads she could handle. Wash and cut, and Dev had stocked up on salad dressing.

Ruth came up beside her. "Come on, Callie. Don't cause problems."

Callie rose from her crouch, brandishing a cucumber. "Why is making salad a problem? I mean I appreciate that Dev is such a good caretaker, but can't we help him out?"

"It's the way things are done here. *Routine is important.*" This last bit was stated with a strange intensity.

Callie eyed her disquieting little sister. "Yeah? Are you

quoting someone there, Ruth?"

"No. It's just the truth. As you know."

Truth? What the fuck? With a sharp shake of her head, Callie gave up talking. Apparently they weren't supposed to talk anyway and given how the conversations went—they gave her a headache—she was beginning to see why. She made her salad though, despite Ruth's occasional noises of distress.

When she was done, Dev came into the kitchen. He looked wiped out, as if he'd been working long, weary hours at a high-stress job. If Callie had known him better she would be concerned. But Callie didn't get concerned about human males like this one who didn't want her around. Even if he had gorgeous eyes.

"What are you doing?" he demanded of her.

She waited, no longer willing to argue with these two unsettling creatures. God, she missed Trey who was the most practical-minded person she had ever met and who *made sense.*

"You can still make the main dish, Dev," Ruth put in quickly, her tone appeasing. "Callie only tossed a salad. Only to be helpful." Her words seemed to reassure Dev, and Callie found she hadn't the heart to try to make something else for dinner in case that unnerved one or both them even further.

So she stepped away from the kitchen and Dev took over cooking.

They ate supper in silence. Madison appeared to find this typical. Ruth was rather blank faced, but perhaps that was the new normal. The official cook had made some tasty Indian food, which didn't exactly go with salad and ranch dressing, but no one seemed to care. Dev glowered while he ate though Callie didn't know who or what had made him angry this time. Finally her sister felt compelled to speak, perhaps because Callie, having given up on the conversation front, had said next to nothing.

"Dev's from India!" This from Ruth.

Dev slowly lifted his gaze from his plate. "I was actually born *here*, Ruth."

"You know what I mean." Ruth rolled her eyes and mouthed "very sensitive" to Callie.

Callie didn't know about sensitive but supposed she should have known Dev was an Indian name. She didn't pay much attention to heritage, given she had only the haziest memories of her mother and no idea where *she* came from. One of her foster parents had decided her amber eyes were from Brazil.

"The food is very good," Callie offered, trying to catch Dev's eye. He gave a curt nod, as if praise was uncalled for, almost ridiculous. "Thank you. It's kind of you—"

"Dev doesn't mind," Ruth cut in.

Okay, why was Ruth speaking for Dev now? It was so odd to see this man looking after her sister. Callie didn't know what to think of it. Fortunately Dev wasn't made resentful by Ruth's remark, though his expression did turn wry.

"Good thing, I guess." Callie scraped her plate clean. "That he doesn't mind," she added when Ruth looked puzzled. "So, what do you do, Ruth?"

"Do?" That blank look again. Callie reacted with some horror, wondering if these blank expressions of Dev and Ruth were catching and she'd be wearing one soon. She rather dreaded the idea of donning such a mask for whatever reason. In addition to horror, though, Callie also felt irritation. She'd never before itched to smack someone upside the head, had considered it a metaphorical expression. Till now, when she regarded her sister.

58

"Well." Callie swallowed the last of her rice. "Dev here seems to cook and do childcare. What's your contribution to the household?"

"Shop," replied Ruth promptly.

"That's funny, because I noticed that Dev went out and brought home all the groceries today."

"Oh, not for food." Ruth's tone suggested that her shopping for food was a silly notion. "For clothes." She rubbed the material of Dev's shirt between her fingers. Callie had the odd impression Dev was trying not to flinch. "Like this T-shirt."

"Shop for clothes." Callie paused. "Anything else? Do you, say, clean the house?"

Ruth became rather sullen and, acting like she'd been caught out, went back to eating.

"We share the chores," put in Dev. His dark eyes conveyed disapproval. Evidently this line of questioning, like all Callie's other conversational gambits, was not welcome. "Though I do more of the work. Ruth's been sick, you see, and she's still recovering."

Callie turned her gaze back to Ruth. Having never seen her sister so healthy in her life—the dark circles under her eyes were gone and Callie recalled again that Ruth wasn't smoking—Callie had to wonder at Dev's statement. "When was she sick?"

Dev shrugged and his expression threatened to go trancelike again. Gawd. Callie cast about for something to say to prevent Dev's zoning out, but then he answered, "A month?" while glancing at Ruth.

"I don't know." Her movements a little jerky, Ruth started clearing the table. She lifted her chin as she announced, "*I* will do the dishes tonight."

"If you want," said Dev, and Ruth gave a definitive nod.

While Callie might have felt some satisfaction in goading her sister to pitch in, the circumstances made it impossible. She sighed and shifted to look out the window, feeling desperate for some fresh air, some open spaces, feeling desperate to get away from this claustrophobic house and its unnerving occupants. "I'm going for a walk. When did you say Scott would get here?" She didn't want to miss his arrival, that's for sure.

Ruth turned back from the sink, eyes lit up with enthusiasm. "He said he was leaving after work. So not till nine or so. Maybe later if the traffic's bad." She smiled. "I can't wait, eh, Dev?"

Dev didn't react.

I can't wait either, Callie thought.

Callie did wait. She also prowled—as human, of course— the streets of the suburb. By the time she returned, it was almost dusk. Madison was in bed and Dev seemed to be haunting the back porch. Probably where he'd been last night when he'd found her.

She chose to walk around to the back of the house quietly, taking the opportunity to observe him. Trey would approve of a little reconnaissance, even if technically it was impolite.

Dev sat on a bench swing, pushing himself back and forth with one foot, staring down at that foot, his face set in stone. It wasn't a good expression and it actually caused Callie some pain. She hadn't cared about anyone but Trey and Ruth for a long time, so these feelings of concern, new as they were, for a strange man and the child in his house, put her on edge. She hadn't meant to think about anyone but Ruth.

With a jerk, Dev stopped pushing the bench and flipped his face up to run a hand over his eyes—a rather despairing gesture that moved Callie.

After blowing out a rough breath, he returned to rocking, the slow creak of the wood mesmerizing Callie. His one arm was stretched out along the top of the bench. She had this desire to nestle under that arm, and imagined Dev pulling her close.

Odd. She was so used to her crush on Trey that it felt awkward to be drawn to someone else. She searched her mind for the reasons for this new and sudden attraction to a human. He was handsome, no doubt, the eyes particularly so. He was fit, muscular, and she liked that. But Callie suspected she was susceptible to these feelings because he looked after Madison and even Ruth, though the latter more grudgingly, she suspected. He often seemed irritated by her sister. Well, so was Callie.

His chest rose and fell, his biceps flexed. He wasn't quite at ease. Neither was she, but Callie decided that she had spent enough time watching him, that this one-sided observation wasn't fair, so she stepped forward, out of shadow, to make her presence known.

He jolted to his feet with a noisy inhale, almost a sound of alarm.

"It's me," she said unnecessarily. She had to speak or be drowned in those large brown eyes made black by the night. She offered him a smile. "Your new and unwanted houseguest, remember?"

His apprehension subsided. If she listened very carefully, she could hear his too-fast heartbeat, but at least the beat was decelerating. She wanted to protect him. That thought hit her with a bit more force than expected. Especially considering the circumstances, in that she didn't properly understand the danger to this house, only that there was one.

So, now she (and Puma) wanted to get Ruth, Madison *and* Dev away from here. First though, she would identify the source of the danger, or at least, to sound a little less dramatic, identify what the hell was wrong. Because something was very wrong.

"You should leave," he said in a low voice. The warning was not a threat, but advice delivered for her sake. Perhaps he believed she was at risk. He couldn't know her hidden strengths, and she didn't intend him to. "Scott looks after Ruth, in his own way. It's not so bad. It could be worse."

Callie stepped towards Dev and she had the impression it took some work on his part to hold his ground.

"Something is bad, Dev, and, what's more, you know it."

He didn't respond and before he could go into a trance— she saw the danger signs, unfocused gaze, tension in the mouth suggesting he was trying to say something yet couldn't—she added, "It's better that I stay and meet Scott. I can take care of myself, you know. I am, as Ruth says, strong."

The short lift of his eyebrows before he looked away conveyed complete doubt. He didn't say anything, just stared off into the distance. After a while he asked, "What were you doing out there last night?" He gestured towards the back of the yard, evidently bemused by recalling how he'd found her in the grass.

How to explain? Well, she couldn't. "I wasn't sure this was the address Ruth was staying at. I didn't want to be thought an intruder."

"But you are."

"I guess so."

"Look." Still gazing out into the dark, the words seemed to be pulled from Dev, like he found speech to be an enormous effort. "Don't let Scott know Madison talks. And don't"—here his voice became even more strained—"ask me why."

"Okay," she said simply.

He faced her again, expression wary. "Really?"

"Really. I like that you want to protect Madison. I want to protect her too."

"And how will you do that?" The faint derision in his voice was dampened by weariness.

"I'm going to confront Scott."

He grimaced and spoke through clenched teeth, the whites of them obvious in the darkness. "There is no point."

She chose not to argue. If she had learned anything this past twenty-four hours, it was that you couldn't argue with these two people in this strange house. Either they said something painfully nonsensical or they spaced out. Leaving her with no argument to win. Not that she wanted to win, she wanted to connect, to Ruth, to Dev.

Despite his unusual behavior, she was drawn to this new human. Maybe *because* he was strange. Given her own freak status, the normality of other men had always made her uneasy.

Instead of speaking, she stepped forward. She watched his face stiffen and realized he was trying to hold his place, not back away. She raised a hand, found she wanted to place it on his chest.

"No," he said, the word flat, and he turned, barely avoiding her touch.

Despite his rebuff, Callie spoke to his back. "I wish you could tell me what is going on here. Ruth makes no sense and I think you know that."

He drew in a long breath, and for a moment she thought he might speak again. Then he silently entered the house, leaving her alone on the porch.

Chapter Five

It was past time to put her excellent hearing to use. So Callie waited on the back porch and was rewarded when, about an hour later, a car pulled into the driveway. She crept around the side of the house, keeping to shadows, but didn't turn the corner. And she listened.

As soon as the car door slammed shut, Ruth was on the front steps calling out, quite joyfully, "Scott!" Callie had little time to be shocked by her sister's enthusiasm before the greeting and its emotion was reciprocated.

"Hey, sweetie." It was actually a nice voice—Callie had expected something more sinister—even if she found the "sweetie" rather cloying. "How are you?"

"Good." A perky word from Ruth.

"It's good to see you." Then, "Mmm."

Callie darted a look around the corner to see they were hugging. Before they could start to make out or even exchange a kiss, Scott placed his hands on Ruth's shoulders and set her apart. He gave a slight squeeze of reassurance before he let go and stepped backwards.

"Where's Dev?" demanded Scott, more businesslike now.

"In his room."

"How is he?"

"The same." Ruth sounded bored, making it clear that discussing Dev did not interest her.

"Overhear any more crying jags?"

Pause. "Last week." Here at least Ruth sounded more troubled.

"Okay. You're not causing him problems, right, Ruth? He's a bit fragile right now."

"No. I'm good. I swear."

Scott huffed out a sigh. "Not sure what I should do about him." Ruth had nothing to offer, so after the silence dragged on, Scott added, "This new development. Your sister?" Voice lowered. "Where is she?"

"Out back."

"I didn't even know you had a sister."

"Foster sister," Ruth acknowledged. "Though she's like a real sister to me. She loves me." This was said with some defiance, and any aggravation Callie had felt towards Ruth completely evaporated.

"I'm sure she does," Scott said soothingly. "You're very lovable. But Ruth." Significant pause and Callie was tempted to peek at them again, but decided not to risk it. "Ruth," he repeated, his tone now stern, "you must tell her to leave."

"Oh." Ruth's voice was small.

"Tell her you are very sorry, you love her, but she just has to leave." Stern words indeed, which pissed Callie off. "Ruth? Respond."

"Yes, I will." She sounded subdued.

Fuck you, buddy, thought Callie, and as they opened the door to the house, she moved swiftly to the back porch.

She didn't know what disturbed her more, Dev's apparent crying jags or Scott's way of interacting with Ruth. As if, well, as

65

if he was in total control of her life. Control freak, Callie decided, and that went in the not-good category. Even if he didn't hit Ruth.

A few minutes later, Ruth poked her head out the back door to peer into the darkness, looking for Callie.

"I'm here." Callie sat on the corner of the porch, arms wrapped around her legs, waiting for what would happen next.

"Callie?" Ruth stepped out, let the screen door swing shut behind her. She approached, her face set, ready to do something unpleasant.

"Was that Scott?" Callie asked innocently. "I heard a car."

"Yes. Scott." Ruth bobbed her head once.

"Where is he now?"

Ruth considered, before she divulged, "He's talking to Dev."

"I thought we weren't supposed to talk, or that rule doesn't apply to Scott?"

Instead of responding, Ruth just scrubbed her face with both hands, then sighed. "Callie?"

"Still here, sis."

She squared her shoulders and looked straight at Callie. "I am very sorry, I love you, but you just have to leave."

The lack of inflection and Scott's exact wording made Callie's skin crawl. She closed her eyes for a moment, gathering her thoughts together and working towards answering in a casual manner. She wasn't going to get in a fight with Ruth, who'd had too many people bully her in her life. "Okay, listen, I won't stay forever, but a few days longer."

While this response made Ruth look less sad, it also seemed to stump her. "But you have to leave." She paused, face going doleful again, took a breath and began, "I'm very sorry—"

"Don't worry." Callie couldn't stand to hear the recitation a second time. "I *will* leave." She actually smiled at Ruth who, to Callie's dismay, burst into tears. She leapt up to give her little sister a hug, rubbing her back. "Don't worry," she repeated. "Okay?"

"But Scott—"

"Tell Scott I'm leaving. Because I am."

Ruth calmed at the advice. "Okay, yeah, okay. You're leaving."

"Yes." *Just not right away.* Callie gave Ruth another squeeze before she led her sister back inside. "Let's go up."

Ruth acquiesced, which was good. Callie wanted to get upstairs and eavesdrop on whatever conversation Scott was having with Dev, who didn't much like to talk. Perhaps Dev became chatty when Scott was around?

Four years ago, she'd been told by Trey that good shifter etiquette meant she shouldn't eavesdrop on everyone at will with, as he dubbed it, her superhearing. She thought he would make an exception here. In fact, she wished she could consult with Trey now. Maybe he could make some sense of this strange household she'd stumbled upon.

"What's going on?" demanded Scott.

Dev didn't answer, he just glared, meeting Scott's gaze, though the eyes had power and it was stupid to tempt the young Minder by looking directly at him. But Dev never could give way on the small things. Just on what was important. Which was why he loathed himself so.

Scott gave an impatient twist of his head. "Don't make me push, Dev. I don't like it. Especially with you."

"Then don't push," Dev replied evenly. He used to take pride in replying without rancor. No more. That said, it was still safer.

"Trouble is, I need to know if this Callie is a threat to us."

"No."

"Truth, Dev."

"*No.*"

"No to truth? No to Callie being a threat?"

"Both."

Scott eyed him, clearly fed-up. Dev didn't care but, of course, Scott would make him care very, very soon. Never mind his small, useless victories, even if they kept him sane.

"You agreed to this, Dev."

Had he? Dev wished that was in the notes he'd written to himself. Obviously he'd never felt confident about the truth or nontruth of *that.*

"Why would I agree to this? How?" Dev knew he shouldn't ask, knew he had asked many times before and could no longer remember the answers.

"I don't have time for this." With a quick movement, Scott whipped out a hand to grab Dev's wrist, and Dev trembled, but stayed still.

"Let fucking go of me."

"I'm not going to push you, you're too fragile."

"I'm not *fragile.*" Dev forced the words out.

"Yes, you're strong," Scott said. The words were patronizing and Dev felt freaked, like he really was weak. "Ruth's not so strong. I'll have to push her, if you won't tell me the truth."

Dev jerked his arm out of Scott's grasp. "There's nothing to say. Callie thinks we're all weird."

"What's her angle?"

"No angle. She's looking out for her little sister. Wants to protect her, I think."

With a shake of his head, Scott dismissed that. "Why now? She's been totally out of the picture. She wasn't even around when Ruth belonged to Eleanor."

Just the name sent wild thoughts tumbling through Dev, but he resisted the chaos, came back to this discussion with Scott, and threw up his arms in a who-knows gesture. "I can't tell you 'why now'. But Callie is genuinely interested in Ruth's well-being."

Scott appeared to consider this a serious possibility. Enough to ask, "Ruth didn't summon Callie here, did she?"

"I don't think so." Dev didn't want Ruth to get in trouble so he added, "Ruth squealed in shock when Callie arrived, as if she wasn't expecting her sister."

That gave Scott some measure of relief. He hated thinking his control wasn't good, Dev knew. Hated to think one of *his* would ask to be rescued.

"Okay, good. I'd have to rethink if I thought Ruth was trying to get out." Here Scott gave Dev a crooked smile. "On the other hand, I know you are trying to get out."

Dev found it hard to catch his breath.

"You need to remember we're doing good work here, Dev."

Oh yeah. Good work. It's just that nothing about it felt *good*. If only he knew what the fuck "good work" was a euphemism for.

"I haven't pushed you, Dev, and I don't want to push you this visit. We should take a break from that." Inwardly, Dev sneered at the "we". Scott made decisions unilaterally. Dev found it hard to fathom how he'd come to be under the thumb of this overgrown teenager. It galled him. "Remember what our goal is?"

Dev detested these kinds of questions, so he didn't answer, and Scott rolled his eyes to indicate that he thought Dev was acting difficult. Then he answered his question himself.

"Our goal is to take in rescues."

Don't argue, don't argue, don't argue. Dev didn't know if Scott was honest here or playing with him. But asking *that* would never lead to answers, would just get Dev in trouble, with Scott or with his own head.

Scott continued, "We make people better, make them forget what they've been through, and then they can leave. Callie's going to mess up Ruth's leave-taking. If Callie cares for her foster sister, she wouldn't want that. Right?"

Dev remembered his sheet. Apparently Ian and Helen had left. Maybe this was truth. Hard to tell.

"You're not shaking," Scott pointed out.

Dev lifted a hand to see that Scott was right. Despite everything, Dev knew enough to remember shaking and trembling. That awful kind of weakness happened after he'd been pushed by Scott.

"How's Madison?" Scott asked and Dev panicked for a moment, fearing Scott had seen through her guise. Dev wanted to protect Madison's young, developing brain from Scott's pushes. Even if Scott saved people, he couldn't seem to resist exercising his influence over them. A Minder, even one who wanted to save people, could not stop himself from pushing. It was his nature.

"Same." Dev managed to sound offhand but Scott's next question suggested that he hadn't completely succeeded.

"Do you remember that I rescued the child?"

Dev frowned, hating the way that sounded like truth. If it was truth, why did he need to hide Madison's real personality from Scott?

"Max didn't like the way she cried all the time. He would have killed her. *I* don't do that."

Dev searched through his memories, trying to sort them out. It felt right, what Scott said, but was that enough, or had Scott planted the idea in his mind earlier?

"Truth, Dev."

"I've grown to hate the word truth."

Scott's face closed and Dev knew he'd made a mistake. Because, oh yes, how could he forget, Scott wanted them to be friends. Scott was lonely. Dev needed to write down that Scott was lonely. He got in trouble when he didn't remember. Got in trouble when Scott sulked. Got *pushed.*

"Forget it, Dev. You think you want to remember the truth, but you don't, not really."

What Dev wanted was Scott out of his room and out of his head, far, *far* away.

"Anyway, don't worry about Callie. Ruth'll get rid of her."

"Except Ruth wants her to stay," Dev said in a low voice. Better if Scott realized what he was up against.

"No. She doesn't. If Callie stays, she too will have to become one of mine. And no matter how much Ruth adores me, she won't want her sister to belong to me. Neither do you. Right, Dev?"

Dev couldn't follow the conversation for much longer. He was getting lost. "It doesn't matter what I want."

"You're wrong, and somewhere in there you know you're wrong." Scott reached out to touch Dev's temple and he flinched. On Scott's face was a look of disgust. "They didn't even touch you, Dev. I intercepted before that. So you owe me, remember? Remember, Dev?"

"No." He was wheezing now, as if that story, that lie, whatever it was, hurt.

"It's okay. Better that you forget it, I suppose." If Scott were a normal person, Dev would think his casual tone forced, but Scott was anything but normal. "I shouldn't bring up the past. It messes with your head. But you get me so angry, making me out to be the bad guy. I'm good, Dev, and we're in this together." Here Scott grabbed Dev's arm and Dev started to tremble as Scott stared into his eyes, demanding something of him. "I'm *good*," Scott repeated. "I protect you."

Dev froze and then, as Scott waited, he slowly nodded.

With that, Scott released him, turned away and walked out the door, something Dev had wanted him to do since he'd entered the room half an hour ago.

He clenched his fists, unclenched them, and tried to order his thoughts. The only thing that came back to him was that it was true, what Scott had said. *I'm good and we're in this together.*

Dev felt a little shaky, so he lay down on the bed to stare at the ceiling while his mind emptied out.

Time passed...

Perhaps the light tapping had gone on for a while, but the noise didn't register until his door slowly inched open. He bolted up to sitting even though he expected the intruder to be Madison, who was always tentative about entering his room. The child sometimes had sleep terrors and needed to be reassured in the middle of the night.

Whereas Scott never entered his room as if he didn't fully belong.

The person Dev stared at now was Callie, the beautiful interloper who was squinting at the bright ceiling light shining in his room. With a glance at his clock, he realized it was three in the morning. He should have been sleeping in the dark. He usually slept in the dark. He must have been exhausted and forgotten to shut the lights.

"Mind if I turn off your light?" she asked, now shading her eyes against the brightness. The hall behind her was dark.

"Go ahead." Two words. Easy to say.

The room dimmed and he ground the heels of his hands into his eyes so they hurt. It relieved some of the pressure.

"What are you doing here?" He wanted her to leave, he wanted her to stay.

"Came to see if you're okay." She hadn't moved closer and he appreciated that.

"Of course I'm okay." Perhaps he imagined the doubt pulsing off her in waves. So she didn't believe him. Didn't matter.

"Bad dream?"

"Yep." Had he been making some noise? He hoped not, though heat flooded through his body. Embarrassment, he identified.

"I couldn't sleep."

"I see."

"Do you?"

Don't answer. There was no answer. He simply stared. At least Callie's warm amber eyes held no power.

"Never mind that question." She slowly stepped towards him. "I have another."

God, he didn't want questions. His brain was full of them and answers were thin on the ground.

"See, I'm worried about Ruth. She told me to leave the house." Callie eyed him. "Are you going to tell me to leave?"

Answerable, so Dev considered that question. Scott wanted Callie gone which meant... Reason enough for...what? There were reasons. Certainly.

He lost his train of thought and simply stared. She was beautiful, Callie. It hurt a little to see her, caused a tightness in his chest, just in front of his heart. That was a fanciful notion. And an odd one, given that he was asexual.

He went still as he realized she was now beside his bed and he hadn't even heard her move. She moved so silently, especially in the dark.

"I'm just going to sit on the floor beside your bed, okay?" She dropped, so he could only make out the shape of her head. "I want us to be quiet though. I have a feeling Scott wouldn't like us talking."

"Scott likes to talk," Dev offered. It seemed like a safe thing to say. "He's good," he felt compelled to add, in case she had taken his first comment as a criticism. Dev didn't criticize Scott.

"Good," she echoed. "I'd ask you what good meant if I thought you would answer."

A searing sensation ripped through Dev, self-contempt, anger. He hated his weakness. *If I thought you would answer.* She understood his weakness, or at least something about it.

"Okay?" asked Callie, apropos of nothing, and nothing seemed okay. Why was she asking? No one had asked him questions for a long time, except for Scott and the Minder didn't count. The silence stretched on and Dev felt uncomfortable.

"I'm tired," he said finally. "I think it's time you leave."

When she didn't move, he explained, "Leave my room. Ruth needs you."

"She does," Callie agreed. But she didn't move and Dev didn't know what she wanted. "I like you, Dev."

Dev sat there, unsure how to respond. He searched for something appropriate and came up with "Thanks."

"You're welcome."

There was a smile in her voice and a part of Dev wanted to reach for her, just a little bit of human contact. Odd thing to desire, when he disliked human contact. He turned to face her, but the words didn't come.

"I don't usually like men," she said, as if explaining herself.

"No?" This interested him, this surprising statement. Perhaps she, too, disliked contact. Wait, he didn't believe that; she'd welcomed her sister's embraces, and hugged her back.

"I like children and my sister, but not many others." Ah, so she liked him as in *like*, not attracted to. That realization made Dev breathe easier. It also, strangely, disappointed him.

"Somehow it's easier to talk in the dark," Callie said. "When you can't see me. Why is that, I wonder?"

"I don't know." Something loosened in him, because a topic of conversation he could engage in had finally arisen. "You're beautiful."

"I am?" Anyone else, anywhere else, would have been fishing for compliments. Callie just sounded curious.

"Well, I think so."

"I'm glad," she whispered.

"But," he added quickly because he didn't want her getting the wrong idea and coming on to him. That kind of encounter and its fallout, he couldn't withstand. "I don't like women. I mean, I'm not attracted to them. I like you. As you like me." Inwardly he winced, wondering how he'd just managed to sound both inane and formal.

"Oh." She seemed to ponder that while she rested her head on one arm, gazing up at him. "You know, Dev, I don't think that's true."

He wasn't sure what she was referring to, but didn't really care. He just saw red. "Don't"—his voice sounded harsh as he leaned forward—"talk to me about truth. Just *don't*. You know *nothing* about it." He tried to see her expression in the dark, but couldn't quite, only those eyes. She hadn't moved. He wanted to shake her for talking about *truth*. Except that would involve laying hands on her.

"I'm trying to learn. About *it*, that is. Though it's hard, under the circumstances." She sounded earnest, even if she didn't know what she was talking about. She also didn't sound offended, despite his outburst about truth. Pushing herself up to standing, she regarded him with a serious air. "I think I should leave now. Give you a break. Sleep well, Dev-with-the-dark-eyes."

He gazed after her as she disappeared through his door. Dev-with-the-dark-eyes. What did that mean? He rubbed his weary *dark* eyes one more time and lay back down, hoping his mind would float away and he could sleep. He did, but it took a half hour, because he kept thinking of Callie and her slender body moving through his room, towards him, away from him, her movements whisper-soft, her voice clean.

Chapter Six

The next morning Callie woke ready to throttle Scott. Her puma could sink her teeth into the back of Scott's neck and shake the life out of him.

The image should have appalled her. She'd never visualized killing a human before, but Scott had enraged her. In any event, Puma would do nothing. *Callie* would. Because she was in the human world. She made a fist, imagining it connecting with Scott's mouth. Trey would be surprised. He'd been shocked to find out how nonviolent she was, given his admittedly few run-ins with other werecougars.

Callie gave her head a shake.

"What?" demanded Ruth, jerking up from sleep to full awake in a very non-Ruth way.

"Nothing."

"You growled, kinda."

"Huh."

Ruth lost interest in the growl, but her gaze became intent and focused on Callie. "Callie, I'm very sorry, I love you, but you just have to leave."

Callie stared back, wondering if her little sister had become Scott's repeater station and just how many more times she would hear this. More puzzling was the question of how Scott exercised this kind of influence over Ruth. Callie uncurled her fists and forced herself to speak as evenly as possible. "We went over this. I *am* leaving." Ruth cast her a look of relief. "Just not immediately." At that, Ruth frowned. "Remember?"

Her sister smoothed out the blanket bunched at her knees, but her brow remained creased. "We talked about this already? What did Scott say?"

"You know what? I'm going to go talk to Scott now, because I haven't even met him yet." Callie was striving for a casual tone, but somehow that came out with a weird kind of strained jocularity to it. Oh well. To avoid further discussion on the topic, Callie bolted from the room.

She made it down to the kitchen to find Dev making breakfast—bacon and eggs. Madison was in the den watching TV, and Scott was in there too. No one paid attention to Callie, though Dev grunted a greeting of some kind, so she just watched Scott who lobbed the occasional question at Madison. The child acted impervious and didn't appear to be aware that Scott was alive, let alone in the same room with her. Madison was acting and that very much intrigued Callie.

On a long sigh, Scott pushed down on his knees and rose from the couch. As he entered the kitchen, he came to a stop at the sight of Callie.

"Good morning." He seemed genuinely surprised to see her, and a little put out. Perhaps he'd expected immediate results from Ruth's request that Callie leave. The fury began to rise in her again, and she resolutely squashed it. This conversation was a scouting mission of sorts, so she intended to do it right.

Therefore Callie nodded at Scott. No harm in her practicing how to be polite to someone she despised. In the future it might become an important social skill. More to the point, she felt the situation in this house was serious yet totally incomprehensible, and she needed to come to a better understanding about what was going on.

"I'm Callie." She held out her hand, but Scott hunched his shoulders and put both hands in his front pockets, obviously unwilling to shake. Callie dropped her arm back down to her side. Examining his face more closely, she saw that he was neither plain nor handsome, rather nondescript. Crew cut. His eyes were gray, cool, but most shocking was his age. She didn't think he was more than twenty. If that. Probably younger than Ruth. Callie had expected someone older to be running the show in this house. Besides, Ruth had always gravitated to older men.

"Find what you're looking for?" Scott drawled and she blinked, unsure of his meaning. "You're looking at me as if you're searching, Callie." He said her name with a kind of creepy intimacy that she disliked.

He was right, she was searching for reasons: why Scott affected Ruth so strongly, why Dev had Madison pretending she didn't talk, and why Scott chatted with Dev about pushing, goals and good works. Because, yes, she'd eavesdropped on their conversation last night, and she hadn't liked what it had done to Dev. Given the strange vibes, she felt no compunction about lying. "You look familiar. Have we met?"

Now Callie had received this line a time or two in her past, usually in some kind of bar and usually delivered with a bit more enthusiasm. Still, Scott reacted not unlike the way she had back then, with a "you've got to be kidding" expression coming over his face. She had a terrible urge to smirk until she caught sight of the tense, strained expression on Dev's face. How could this young man possibly have such a terrible hold on Dev? Callie couldn't comprehend it. Or had she misunderstood Dev's character?

"Hey, Callie." Dev used casual words, but no casual tone. "I thought Ruth said you were leaving."

"Oh, I am." She nodded vigorously and both men relaxed. "In a few days." The men tensed again. She reached over and snagged a piece of freshly cooked bacon, crunched on it.

"Callie." Scott spoke her name slowly, drawing out the "L" sound, and stepped towards her, his expression intent. "You—"

"Ruth," blared Dev, shouting right into them, even though Ruth was upstairs, and Callie winced at the noise. "*Breakfast!*"

Scott rolled his eyes. "Turn down the foghorn, Dev, do you mind?"

Dev responded with a weird urgency. "Everything's fresh. We might as well eat now. Callie, maybe you should go tell Ruth breakfast is ready." The hint of desperation in Dev's voice disturbed Callie and she turned to glare at Scott.

Scott pointed a finger a Dev. "Shut up for a minute, you." Then, to Callie, finger included, "Pack your bags and leave."

Bite me. She didn't say it, not a good idea. "I will. Just, not today."

Scott cocked his head, eyes suddenly lit with interest and some alarm. "Callie, I have a question for you." From behind Scott, Callie could see Dev shaking his head at her, warning her as Scott continued, "Why *wouldn't* you leave today?"

"Because I have to look after my sister."

"That's a very strong drive of yours, is it?"

Strange way to put it, but Callie answered, "I suppose that's true, yes."

"Okay…" He grabbed her forearm, which was at odds with his earlier hands-off attitude, and stared deeply into her eyes, like how one would gaze into a lover's eyes. Callie was repulsed. "Callie, drop to the floor and do fifty pushups. Not here," he added as she glanced down at the kitchen's linoleum. "In the den."

She withdrew her arm from his grasp and considered the situation, moving her gaze back and forth between the two men. Dev seemed puzzled whereas Scott radiated tension and doubt. Even fear. While Callie had no desire whatsoever to follow any directive of Scott's, her gut told her to do it, to pretend Scott had control over her, as a way to understand what control he actually did have over Ruth and Dev.

God knows that talking to Ruth and Dev had thus far not revealed much of the situation to Callie. She went with her gut.

"Okay." Callie smiled, deciding to add a bright attitude to her demeanor, given that everyone was acting, and these were the silliest orders she'd ever received. She slid her gaze past a troubled Dev to Scott, who looked...relieved. How would this peculiar young man have reacted if she'd refused to obey?

Now was not the time to find out. Instead, she walked into the den, giving her step a little bounce, then dropped to the floor and started the pushups. Human women were often unable to do pushups for any length of time unless they worked on their upper-arm strength. Given that Callie had spent over half her life on all fours, this was a not her problem, and the exercise was a breeze. She was aware of Scott standing at the threshold of the den, watching her short workout. Once he left at the twelfth pushup, Callie let herself glance up at Madison, whose too-serious gaze rested on her. Callie winked as if they shared a secret, and reassured, Madison returned the wink.

Dev didn't know what to make of it. Callie, by refusing to leave Ruth, seemed to outright disobey Scott, which he'd never observed before. Going by his reaction, neither had Scott. Then when given another directive, Callie without any of those muddled looks first-time people usually got, bounced off to the den and executed fifty pushups.

Maybe Callie would find it easier to be a member of this "coterie"—Scott's favorite word since he disliked the term zombie—than some would. Maybe obeying Scott—well, when she did—would go easier on her than on Dev. Though he couldn't quite wish that lack of will on her.

She should have left the house, but Dev had lost the ability—he sneered at himself—to even warn her off. He didn't have the strength to do anything but "good work". Whatever the fuck that meant.

Ruth had been his good work this last month or two months, however long it had been. Dev did recall her appearance when she'd arrived—high, skeletal skinny, bruises, walking like it hurt, a fucking mess. And look at her now. She was happy, sometimes.

Or was that Scott talking? Scott talking about rescues and making people healthy.

Dev shook himself, trying to stop this internal monologue that ran around his head in circles till he started feeling crazy. What he had to do was clean up the kitchen and get Madison out of the house, away from the TV and Scott—the combination was going to make *her* a zombie and that was the last thing he wanted. Bad enough for an adult, but kids... Dev feared the brain damage caused by a Minder's influence would be irreversible for a child.

He stalked into the den and Madison jerked her head around.

"Let's go for a bike ride, Mad."

She slid a knowing finger to her face, placing it directly over her lips to indicate she was staying silent. Then she jumped up, put on her shoes and Dev followed her out to the garage.

He didn't want to think about what Scott was doing with Ruth. "Earning her trust", he supposed. Problem was, Scott's trust issues were unlike most other people's. He didn't trust, and he didn't deserve to be trusted. Not anymore.

"Callie did fifty pushups. I counted." Madison sounded impressed and her voice brought Dev back to the present. They were outside, down the street, and he couldn't remember leaving the garage, let alone walking down the sidewalk. How long had they been outside? He ground his teeth, but refused to be drawn into the anger and confusion that came with memory lapses. Instead, he watched Madison who was about to get back on her bike, and he was about to run beside her again. He sometimes got so caught in his head, spinning around the same thoughts again and again, that he worried about finding his way out. Madison's presence in his life actually helped, and if he weren't so concerned about her safety, he might have been thankful for her living with him.

"She did," Dev agreed. Not sparkling conversation and a bit of time lag, but the great thing about Madison was she didn't mind as long as Dev was there and said something eventually.

"Can you do fifty pushups?"

"In fact, I can." Dev seemed to think the fitter he was, the better he could defend himself. The idea of defending himself was a joke, but still he ran, he lifted weights and, yes, he did pushups.

"Can you teach me? I want to learn how to do them."

"Sure. They're not complicated. But wait until Scott's gone, okay?" He didn't like Madison to do anything that might catch Scott's interest and give her away.

Madison pouted, almost a scowl.

"Better that way, Mad. Okay?" He put a hand on her shoulder.

She immediately leaned into him, practically falling off her bike in her desire for a hug. He felt guilty. Small children needed touch. He knew that, but tended to forget because of his own predilection to avoid touch. Madison, unlike anyone else, he didn't mind contact with. So despite the fact it was awkward as hell given his half-crouch, and it caused her bike to clatter to the ground, he drew her into a big bear hug. She nestled there for a while, her small body soaking up affection until she got restless.

Finally she squirmed out of his hold. "It's boring when Scott's here. Why's he staying so long?"

"It's good for him, to get away."

"Away from what?"

"From his other home." Dev gave a sharp shake of his head. He tried not to think of Scott's other home and besides, it was the wrong conversation to have with the child. Fortunately she moved on to the next question. "Where's your bike, Dev?"

"In the garage." He wasn't quite sure where this was going.

"I want you to bike with me," she announced, her chin raised in decision.

"Okay." He scratched his jaw and noticed that he needed to shave. He forgot that sometimes too. He hated all the things he forgot. "One problem. You'll need to bike on your own then. I can't hold on to your bike and ride my own."

"I know that." Her tone implied he was silly to think she'd overlooked this important fact. "I'm ready."

"Sure?" Dev had gotten rather used to always keeping his hand on her bike seat. He gamely ran along, and after she started yelling for him to let go, he did.

It was just as much work to run beside Madison, with his arms outstretched ready to catch her now-wobbly bike. She kept her balance and the wobble smoothed out and he found he was smiling as he jogged down the road with her.

Later Dev went for a run on his own. Scott even encouraged the activity, which made Dev a bit uneasy. Still, he was pretty sure it was his own compulsion, not Scott's, that drove him to exercise.

After his run, he peeked into the den to see Callie playing cards with Madison in silence. That was okay. Scott thought it normal that Madison liked anything with numbers, and cards had numbers. Thank God Scott wasn't seriously interested in Madison.

Dev showered and, as he got dressed, heard the vacuum cleaner start up. Odd. Despite what Dev had told Callie earlier, Ruth rarely did housework. At first, Ruth had been too sick to do anything and now she had little inclination. She was young, a bit of a slob, and lazy. Dev couldn't give a shit. He didn't have much to do anyway and God knew he needed to keep busy. He used to have a life... *No, just don't go there.* It solved nothing to dwell on the past. There was even a reason he was here, if he ever remembered it.

When Dev descended, because he knew Scott would want his company, he saw it was Callie vacuuming. As he stepped into the living room, she switched off the motor.

"Good run?" she asked.

Easy to answer. "Yes." He tried to move away, because he just didn't want to get caught by one of her questions. Besides, the way she watched him set his teeth on edge.

"I'm going for a run later today. Sometime we should run together."

He nodded. Noncommittal.

"But"—her voice took on a forced bright tone—"first I have to vacuum. Because *Scott* said I should. What do you think of that?"

Here he did feel caught. Shit. He hated it when the wheels started spinning and he couldn't find an answer or even an appropriate response. His mind became this hamster running on an endless wheel and he didn't know how to get off.

"Never mind," she put in hurriedly. "I didn't ask that. I meant to say, I think it's great." At his baffled look—he couldn't remember what she was talking about, what was great—she added, "Me doing chores. It's like I've become part of this household or something." She lifted her shoulders in an exaggerated shrug and turned the vacuum back on.

Strange, thought Dev, watching her. She didn't seem to be much different than this morning, before Scott had pushed her. Now it was true, memories, at least Dev's, were problematic. Yet he could have sworn that it was an adjustment, a strain, to be forced to obey a Minder. It *cost* a body.

But maybe, just maybe, it didn't cost Callie. Maybe she'd be able to leave.

The melody of "Hotel California" drifted through his mind and Dev could only think for the hundredth time that he *loathed* that song.

"Dev," called Scott from the kitchen. No push behind it, but the threat of a push was more than enough to propel Dev towards his Minder.

Chapter Seven

Supper was an odd affair. Callie remained upbeat, even after Scott kept talking to her, pushing her. Dev could tell her manner rattled Scott, as he had Callie washing the dishes, mopping the floor, cutting the grass in the backyard.

She did it without blinking, giving Ruth occasional hugs, because Scott's focus on Callie was making Ruth nervous, even jealous. Dev had often wondered just how much of Ruth's crush on Scott was Scott and how much was Ruth. Not that it would go beyond that, given the Minder's past.

"I hope we can be good friends," Scott told Callie as Dev led Madison up to bed.

Dev didn't wait to overhear her response. The bitterness flooding him over the word "friend" was too much to bear. Foolish Ruth, calling her sister here. Dev would never have betrayed one of his family in that way and brought them into this nightmare. However, Ruth was young and lost, and it was hard to muster a lot of anger towards her.

That night Dev stared at the ceiling. Madison was in bed, asleep he hoped, although she had whispered questions at him. Well, the same question. Namely, "When is Scott going to leave?"

Scott visited often, and rarely stayed more than one night. Right now he didn't seem in any hurry to leave. And why was that?

He wanted to gain Callie's trust, since she'd "decided" to become one of the coterie. Ruth was thrilled, or you might think she was thrilled by her enthusiasm, if you didn't notice the edge of nervousness.

Dev had yet to figure out if Ruth was trying to get out from under Scott's influence by bringing her sister in.

Or not. He blinked, testing his thoughts. They weren't too disjointed tonight, which implied that Scott hadn't pushed much today. Scott claimed he didn't want to push Dev at all, but no matter how far gone Dev was, he knew not to trust that claim. Despite Scott's desire to be deemed "good", in his own mind and in the minds of others, he could never resist using his powers.

Dev turned away from thoughts of Scott, desperate to think of someone else. Like Callie who had visited him in the middle of the night. He found himself wondering if she'd return. It might actually have been hope, though he had a hard time identifying the emotion, it had been so long.

But no, now he remembered. Scott had eyed Callie with some suspicion before telling her she was not to talk to Dev. After that push, she wouldn't be entering his bedroom tonight.

Dev turned onto his side and pillowed his head on his arm. It didn't really matter. He couldn't even engage in a coherent conversation. She'd already cottoned on to that fact, given that she hastily answered her own questions whenever Dev got stuck trying to respond to something she'd said.

He had nothing to offer her but despair. And good cooking.

He must have dozed, because he didn't notice the door opening, only it closing, and her shadow gliding towards him.

"Dev?" A bare whisper. He didn't move, just stared, wondering how she could be in here after Scott's directive. She must have a strong drive to visit Dev, then, and he tried to fathom why that would be so. It was very strange, and hope, that strange, foreign creature, leapt in his chest again.

He couldn't show it. Couldn't show anything. Scott wouldn't like it. They had to pretend and protect, all for doing good work. There was a reason for this. A reason... A gray hand appeared in his line of vision, waving in the near darkness. He couldn't see well, but he could see enough for Callie to draw his attention back to her.

"Your eyes are open."

"Yeah," he admitted. Easy response.

"I thought you might be sleeping with your eyes open, because you didn't seem to notice me."

"I noticed you, I just..." *Get lost in my head. All the fucking time.*

"Don't explain." She dropped into a crouch, placing crossed arms on the edge of his bed, propping her chin on those long, graceful arms, and gazing at him. It was night, but the streetlight allowed him to see her face, if not terribly clearly. He had the impression she could see everything about him. Good thing he'd kept his boxers on, despite the heat. Not that it mattered. It wouldn't, to an asexual.

He liked her presence, liked the way she smelled cool and fresh, the way she tilted her head to the side. Her mess of hair that should have looked unkempt, but instead was attractive.

The word *sexy* floated through his brain, but he dismissed it until, with a shock of recognition, he realized his dick was hard and he jolted up to sitting.

"What?" she asked, careful not to move. He'd been perspiring from the heat, but unlike most men, his odor appealed to her. She couldn't describe it except warm, male, even welcoming. Not that Dev would actually welcome her getting closer. At least right now.

He was tense again. He hadn't been for a moment there. She would have liked to crawl into bed with him and bury herself into his sheets, into the smell of him. But men didn't like to cuddle. They just liked to fuck.

Then again, Dev was different. He cooked, he looked after small girls, he went into trances. Maybe he didn't just fuck women.

Not that he was interested in her that way. He obviously had bigger worries, given this household and its strange rules.

He sat with his knees up, arms resting on his legs, and he seemed...surprised, perhaps.

"Something happen?" she asked.

"No," he denied quickly, despite the fact that he appeared to be on high alert. "Why are you here?"

She chose her words with some care. "Scott kept me busy today, but I like talking to you." When he didn't answer, she added, "Is that okay? That I like to talk to you?"

His gaze rested on her, giving little away. "You shouldn't." Oh dear, he was reverting back to those dire warnings of his. Not the most interesting thing about him, even if there was a part of her that warmed to the concern that inspired it.

She decided to explore what he meant. "I shouldn't talk to you because of Scott?"

He swallowed and when he spoke, he seemed to have some difficulty getting the words out. "You should go."

"Do you want me to go?"

His gaze went diffuse, presaging that trancelike state he entered when she asked a question that caused him some difficulty. She could jump past it, by answering herself or simply changing the subject. This time she decided to wait it out. Because he wasn't very close to her—he now sat on the opposite side of the bed—she pulled herself up onto the mattress, crossed her legs, and leaned back against the headboard. A good two feet lay between them, but at least they could sit at eye level.

He watched her closely.

She'd seen revulsion in men before. Trey had warned her that one of the gifts and pitfalls of being a shifter was having extraordinary senses. It was easy to pick up reactions humans might not. As a wolf, Trey's special gift had been smell. Puma, on the other hand, gave Callie keen eyesight and hearing.

Dev wasn't repulsed by her joining him on the bed, but there was some kind of strain. His body was tense, shoulders stiff, hands clenched.

"No." The word was a bare murmur and it took a moment to realize he was answering her question, *Do you want me to go?* She smiled, but he didn't. Even in the darkness Callie could see that his answer was a confession of sorts, something that embarrassed Dev and heated his cheeks with the flush of blood. "But you should leave. Safer."

He glanced away then, his face twisting.

"Safer for who? You, Dev?" She didn't want to make it worse for him.

He shook his head. "You. Get away from Scott." The words seemed wrung from him, as if they cost him effort to speak.

She could make out the slightest vibration in his body and she didn't like it. "You know, I don't like Scott much."

"He's not all bad," Dev said immediately. It sounded like some kind of standard reply, but Callie couldn't imagine very many people discussed Scott with Dev. Her appearance and her questions seemed to have placed the household in disarray.

"People rarely are all bad." She thought that was a nicely diplomatic reply. "I'd like to understand him better."

"You *can't*."

"I'll try then. How did you meet Scott?"

It took a long time for Dev to do whatever he did with his brain while he searched for a response. Callie listened to the night insects, crickets mostly, and the rustling of leaves that came with the soft breeze.

Dev's breath shuddered out. "I used to...look after him. Sometimes. When he was younger."

"You sure?"

"Yes." He didn't sound sure at all.

"I'd guess that Scott's ten years younger than you, no? Did you babysit him or something?"

He rubbed his mouth. "Or something."

"I don't understand."

"I used to look after Scott," he repeated wearily with an air of defeat, and she decided that she wouldn't ask any more questions. Besides, she didn't know what to do with the answers, and the questions hurt the dark-eyed man who sat on the bed with her.

"I like you, Dev."

That had him jerking his head up. "Don't bother."

"No?" She fought the sinking sensation in her stomach. After all, her investigation into Ruth's situation was not about her attraction to Dev. She was used to this kind of disappointment, to one-sided crushes. In fact, Trey would never have allowed such a declaration on her part. He hadn't allowed any kind of small talk.

Still, she felt a connection to Dev. Maybe because he was the only other semi-sane adult in the house. Connections, in her experience were rare, so it was a little painful to be told not to bother.

"I, uh, I'm not interested." At her frown, he elaborated, "In sex. Never have been." He gave a lopsided smile that reassured her in its odd way. She suspected that in other situations, he could be charming.

"Oh," she said, eager to reassure him that she had no expectations. These night visits with their whispered words were special in and of themselves. "Then we're a good pair. I don't even like sex."

That had him raising his eyebrows. "You don't?" He found this curious. Then, as if something turned over in his mind, his expression became grave. "Something bad happen?"

"Oh no." Another benefit of being a shifter. Her natural strength made it unlikely she'd be forced into bed by a normal man. "It's just me. The way I am." Why was she talking like this? About herself. She was supposed to be trying to understand Dev's relationship with Scott, to understand Scott. Still the words tumbled out. Perhaps because no man had ever told her, while in bed with her, that they weren't interested in sex. The novelty intrigued her. "It's uncomfortable."

"Uncomfortable? The sex, you mean?"

"Well yes." Wasn't that what they were talking about?

He winced. "It shouldn't be *uncomfortable*, Callie."

"That's because you're a guy."

His gaze became very intent, warming her. "No." Dev sounded so sure of himself, and he didn't usually.

"But..." The guys she'd bedded had never seemed uncomfortable to her, but what did she know? "So what about you, why don't you like sex?"

"I'm not interested in sex, Callie. There's a difference." He shrugged. "No sexual drive. Don't particularly like physical contact, you see."

Callie frowned, remembering the way Madison nestled into Dev. He certainly didn't recoil from the child's touch. Maybe he meant *sexual* contact. Her heart rate sped up, even though it was stupid to hope for that kind of connection.

She became so lost in this idea she didn't realize Dev's focus had gone diffuse again, as though caught by the thoughts spinning in his head. At his blank expression, an expression she had begun to blame on Scott, a thought struck her, and she stared at Dev's profile. Strong nose and jaw. Short cropped hair. Deep-set eyes.

She had this awful thought that Scott could have told Dev he didn't like touch and by the telling of it, the concept had sunk so far into Dev that he believed it. She didn't understand how Scott worked, but she understood enough to know he worked something on Dev with his words. How deep did that influence run? What would be the point of telling Dev he wasn't interested in sex? Sometimes when Dev gazed at her, Callie had thought he *was* interested. But she didn't have a lot of experience.

She decided to wait Dev out and let him speak after his admission, rather than turn the conversation away from it. Long minutes passed and she hoped it wasn't too painful to be in his head.

"Callie." His voice sounded strangely thick, and she liked the way he said her name, like it meant something to him. The idea sent a frisson through her. "You should only have sex with someone you like, who can make you comfortable, right?" His question suggested she might find this statement obvious.

Given that she was never comfortable with humans and the only shifter she'd known had shown zero interest in bedding her, that hadn't been possible.

"Okay," she agreed to ease his concern. It was easy to talk in the dark, where she could tell by his expression that he couldn't see her face clearly. "But I'm not usually comfortable with men."

He just gazed at her, at a loss.

"For example, Scott. I don't like Scott."

"Scott doesn't count," he declared harshly. "Scott's in trouble."

"In trouble, or trouble?"

"Both."

She should ask for clarification, and she might have, if she'd thought Dev able to supply her with more. But she was unwilling to send Dev off into another trance. She feared it harmed him and there'd already been too many trance-inducing questions this conversation.

Feeling weary after a day of doing as Scott asked and everyone thinking this was just the normal course of action for her, Callie yawned.

"Time for bed?" Dev gave her a faint smile.

She wanted to ask if she could stay here, but it was difficult to say the words out loud. She hated rejection.

He spoke into her silence. "Is Ruth hard to sleep with?"

"She's usually a restless sleeper. Moves around a lot."

"Sounds like me."

Callie nodded. That was close enough to a dismissal for her. Still she crawled across the bed towards Dev, watched his pupils dilate—a sign of arousal. So he could be aroused, but still not like sex. *Want* sex, she corrected herself. She was the

95

one who didn't like sex. If anyone knew there was a difference between like and want, she did. Or she wouldn't have ended up in bed with strangers.

She knew it would be an odd gesture for him, but she couldn't stop herself. She rubbed her cheek against his knee, catlike, though she really wanted to burrow into his chest, his throat.

"Good night." She pushed off the bed, figuring that if he hadn't recoiled, that was something.

"Good night, Callie," he murmured as she slipped out the door.

She crossed the hall and slid back into bed beside Ruth, whose restlessness of the past two nights had mysteriously vanished. Right now her little sister slept like she hadn't a care in the world. Her face relaxed, she lay on her back, one arm flung behind her head, the other by her side.

With a shiver, Callie recalled how Scott had bid Ruth good night.

"Sleep well, Ruth," he'd said, like it was a chore she had to undertake for his sake, "and sleep deeply. You *need* your rest."

"Yes," Ruth had agreed with a strange fervor, and while Callie had been eavesdropping and out of sight, she could just imagine Scott gripping Ruth's arm or shoulder while staring intently into her eyes. It was his modus operandi. Callie shook out her own arm, remembering his hand on her.

And now, magically, Ruth the light and uneasy sleeper was restless no more. It made Callie sick. Although what evil person insisted that their victims get a good night's sleep?

Callie lay back, hands behind her head and tried to put the puzzle pieces together. Scott with his words and looks, Madison with her silence, Dev with his trances and tension, and Ruth— whose admittedly flighty personality had turned downright inconsistent.

No one would believe Callie if she went to them saying Scott had some kind of power over these people. Then again, no one would believe she was a shifter. Both were true. She knew it in her bones.

Trey came to mind and she wondered what he'd make of it all. She might have to go to him, but she wanted to present him with something more substantial than two days of observation. She'd already failed before his very eyes, practically getting herself killed and putting him at mortal risk while he'd destroyed that feral cougar. She didn't want to fail Trey again. Her need to impress him wasn't entirely healthy, but it was there, and if it pushed her to get some real evidence here, well, that was a good thing.

You didn't just call someone up months after they'd fired you and talk as if you'd discovered a control freak. You needed proof when presenting the unbelievable. She'd shifted in front of Trey to demonstrate she was a werecougar, as he had shifted in front of her. This power of Scott's was more subtle. Unlike that last young cougar, Scott wasn't a feral shifter tearing people's bodies to shreds. Yet Callie had begun to suspect he might be just as dangerous. Because, unless she was very much off the mark, Ruth and Dev were barely holding it together.

Chapter Eight

After tossing and turning beside a dead-to-the-world Ruth, Callie finally fell asleep, and the next morning woke later than she'd planned. She'd wanted to be up and about before Scott, wanted to overhear everything he said. But he was already downstairs.

As was Dev, who moved around in the kitchen and, from the sounds of it, prepared breakfast. No surprise there. What was it Ruth had said? Routine was important. Words to live by, evidently. At least in the House of Scott.

Callie jumped out of bed, pulled on one of Ruth's shirts and a pair of shorts, and walked quietly down to sit on the bottom stair. Truth was, she felt indignant on Dev's behalf. Why did he always have to cook? Couldn't Scott? Or even Ruth?

"Why don't you put blueberries in the pancakes?" Scott's suggestion.

"Sure." Dev's word, uninflected. Callie found she was bracing herself, worried Scott was going to give directives that would harm Dev.

Madison trotted downstairs past Callie, tiny finger raised to lips. Callie imitated the gesture, and cupped an ear to indicate she was listening in. That earned Callie a small, approving smile—she suspected Madison spent a lot of time listening too—and the child leaned over for a hug that Callie returned before

Madison skipped down the hall to the kitchen. Moments later the TV went on. Dev and Madison didn't seem to talk to each other when Scott was around.

"What do you think of this Callie?" Scott murmured, not intending to be overheard.

Pause. "She's good." Callie could hear Dev's tension.

"Good in what way?"

A pan banged down on the stove. "Just *good*."

"Dev." The warning in Scott's voice made the hairs on the back Callie's neck rise. Not literally, it was a puma sensation, but it put her on full alert. Puma sensed danger. She crept forward. If necessary, she would intervene. "Dev, you haven't told her about me, have you?"

"*No.*" The sound of vigorous egg beating. "It's not allowed, so how the fuck could I, Scott?" Vicious, low words.

"You could if she's like me and forced you to speak."

"Like you?" Panic there now. Callie wanted to reach out and assure Dev she was *nothing* like Scott. "What do you mean? All you Minders know each other, keep tabs on each other. You're a *pod*."

Pod? Sounded sinister.

"In our area, yes. She's not from here. God knows where she is from. I find her a mystery." Scott's tone became confiding. "You see, I'm not entirely sure she's under my sway. That's never happened to me before. I usually have good control. Except with another Minder."

"No." Dev's denial was flat, definite, but the strain in his voice indicated he was trying too hard to convince Scott. He would probably hear that because, despite his flaws, Scott was observant. "That's not it. She's not like you."

"Why would you say that, Dev?"

"Because."

"I'm waiting to hear your reason."

"Because." Callie heard Dev's deep breath. "She doesn't make me sick."

Very long pause. "Well, that certainly puts me in my place, doesn't it? I make you *sick*, do I?" Now Scott sounded young and a little whiny. It was almost a relief to hear Scott act his age. He didn't seem invulnerable then. "Even though you'd be dead without me, Dev. Even though I only push you when I absolutely have to."

Callie didn't actually need to be right by the door to hear them now. Scott's voice was rising with every word.

"I thought you were my friend, Dev." The simmering violence alarmed Callie. She'd heard that before, in the voices of Ruth's ex-boyfriends.

On cue, Ruth's feet hit the floor above, then she was running down the hall, down the stairs. Callie pulled back so Scott wouldn't see her, but that precaution soon proved useless because Ruth called out rather belligerently, "Callie, what are you doing lurking outside the kitchen?"

Callie just looked at her sister who said, "What? You shouldn't be eavesdropping. Scott doesn't like it." Head high, Ruth strode by Callie into the kitchen. "Do you, Scott?"

Callie followed Ruth in to find Scott glowering, furious and, she observed, a little afraid of her. Perhaps he thought she would try to control him? Well, if she were one of these "Minders" she sure as hell would. But she was only a rare puma. Ready to tear his fucking throat out.

Callie glanced over at Dev whose knuckles were white as he gripped the handle of the frying pan. She walked to him. Touched the hand, noted the flinch and said, gently, "Let me have that."

"Why?"

"I'm going to cook this morning."

"Callie." Scott was using his command voice. So irritating. She simply hated the way he said her name. Repeatedly. "Leave Dev alone. Come here. To me."

Callie cocked her head, fed up but curious about his next move, so she did as ordered. Scott had the presumption to place a hand on her chin and grip too tight. His touch was unpleasant, fingers pressed against her jawbone. Though she tried to suppress her shudder, she didn't quite succeed.

"Scott, no." Dev scraped out the words past his throat, making it sound like he was fighting something within himself. Then he walked over, grabbed Scott's arm and forced Scott to release Callie.

Scott gaped at this action, and when he spoke, there was a bravado there that belied his scornful attitude. "What's the matter, Dev? Did she tell you to protect her?"

Dev's gaze slid away from Scott who yelled, "*Look at me.*"

Dev jerked his head back, burning eyes wide, full on Scott. Callie had the terrible feeling this made him even more exposed.

"It's not what you think," Callie put in, not entirely sure what Scott *was* thinking, but she sure as hell wasn't a Minder.

Scott didn't take his focus off Dev. In the background, Callie could hear that Ruth had begun to sob, but all Callie's instincts told her she had to protect Dev now. Her sister was not at risk at this very moment, and Ruth, Callie could comfort later.

"You're mine." Scott looked deranged, like he was trying to bore holes into Dev who just stiffened and nodded jerkily. Yet Callie had the impression Dev seethed within. "*Say it, Dev.*"

"Yours." A bare mutter that had Dev shaking and Callie

recoiled. This could not go on.

"Not hers. You will never belong to *Callie*." Scott spat out her name. "You nod"—Callie was disturbed that Dev was nodding again—"but I need you to prove it."

Dev's fists balled and his heart rate sped way up. She could hear it galloping along.

"Hit her, Dev."

Callie watched, horrified, fascinated, as Dev's eyes went shiny and dark. His arm rose, fist tight and white knuckled.

"Hit her, Dev." There was alarm there the second time Scott gave the order, as if he'd expected Dev to have obeyed by now. "Why don't you want to? You're mine."

"I'm yours," Dev repeated desperately. His teeth clenched and he ground the words out. "But I don't want to. You know that counts. *Stop, Scott.*"

Dev was vibrating from the effort of holding back, and Callie had had enough. As Scott opened his mouth, she clenched her own fist and drove it into Scott's temple. Hard. He dropped like a rock while Callie bit down on the pain in her hand. She walked around him as she shook out that stinging hand and Ruth screamed.

Dev was staring at his own clenched fist like it didn't belong to him, and Callie wondered if he was still going to use it. With her unbruised hand, she reached for him, wrapping her hand around his fist to lower it. She unrolled his fingers and very briefly linked her fingers with his, then let go.

"What the fuck is going on?" he asked through chattering teeth, his voice a rasp.

Callie didn't know what to say. She didn't know much beyond one thing. "I am *sick* of listening to Scott talk. His orders are getting on my nerves. They make me want to puke."

Thankfully Ruth stopped screaming, dialed down to weeping, and staggered over to Scott's side. He moaned and rolled around on the linoleum, and Callie realized he wouldn't be out for long. She grabbed a dishtowel, stuffed the cloth in Scott's awful mouth, and batted away Ruth's ineffectual hands as her sister tried to stop her.

Picking Scott up, Callie threw him over her shoulder and carried him down the hall. It was obviously past time for someone to be isolated from the others. *Time out*, she thought grimly as she marched up the stairs.

For a while, Dev just concentrated on breathing. That seemed doable given that his brain had shut down. In the background, he was aware of Ruth huddled on the floor sobbing, but it wasn't until he felt someone tugging his shirt that he came back to the here and now.

Big blue eyes stared up at him. Madison. She didn't say anything, just raised her arms in an entreaty to be lifted up and comforted.

He could do that.

She clung, face turned into the crook between neck and shoulder, small hands tight on his arms, and he couldn't even say it would be okay. Mainly because he didn't know what the hell had just happened. He felt a kind of relief, but also dread, because while he desperately needed Scott out of his life, out of his head, he also knew any replacement would be worse. It was why he didn't fight harder against Scott's hold.

"Is Scott gone?" Madison whispered.

"I don't think so."

"I saw Callie take him away." This said with some approval.

"Yeah." Dev shifted Madison to one arm. He couldn't even

talk about that scene. It sent him spinning. He focused on more immediate needs. "Hey, you must be hungry. Why don't I cook these pancakes?"

"I'm not hungry."

"You still have to eat, Mad. You're a growing girl."

So, Dev juggled pancakes and Madison, and ignored Ruth sitting in the corner. His mind settled down a little, enough to briefly consider throwing Madison and Ruth in the car and taking off.

Of course, he had no ID, no source of money. He'd given that all to Scott, and Dev couldn't go back to his family because... There was a reason there, but he couldn't find it.

Perhaps Callie would prove more harmful than Scott, but Dev couldn't quite believe she had snowed him so completely. To think he'd been worried for her, that she'd stumbled upon a Minder in an attempt to help her sister. Maybe that was a ploy and Scott... God, he couldn't even think about Scott right now.

"Ruth, get up." At Callie's sharp voice, Dev spun around, startled by her reappearance. She moved too quietly. It hadn't taken her long to take Scott away.

She was a threat. Dev had to accept that, though he'd thought Callie was different. Those middle-of-the-night visits had meant something to him, even if he understood he was desperate to have a friend. Someone to talk to when he wasn't supposed to talk, someone who couldn't get inside his head. She'd fooled him. She was one of *them* and had evidently staged a coup. Perhaps she'd even handed over her sister Ruth to Eleanor.

At the memory of Eleanor, Dev shuddered.

"Ruth, please." Her voice was less sharp now, and Callie glanced Dev's way for a moment before walking over to Ruth with a look of resignation. "Get up. At least sit on a chair."

Ruth didn't budge. In fact, she glared at Callie with some belligerence, as if she was a sister Ruth didn't intend to listen to. As if Callie wasn't a Minder.

Dev carefully set Madison down, because he was afraid he might drop her.

"What are you?" he demanded as Callie crouched beside her sister.

Her amber gaze turned to hold his, and expecting an order, he tried not to flinch. "I'm a cougar," she said.

He let out a breath of relief. That was no command. A nonsensical statement, but no demand in it, nothing he was supposed to do or think. As she kept looking at him, expecting a response, he began to doubt this idea of his that she was a Minder. "Cougar?"

"Yep. I don't want to talk about it."

Sex is uncomfortable and she's a cougar, an older woman who goes after younger men? These statements of hers didn't exactly add up. Then again, nothing in his life did. "I don't think you're even old enough to be a cougar."

"Any age." Another nonsense response that wasn't an order, and stated matter-of-factly while she raised Ruth to standing and guided her to a chair. Ruth was still crying, though quietly now, thank God. With Ruth settled, Callie sat beside her, apparently overwhelmed. "Why's my sister crying, Dev? And why are you shaking? And why does Madison pretend to be autistic? I mean *what the hell is going on* and how does Scott control you?"

As soon as the words were out—no orders in any of them, only questions and bafflement—Callie darted a gaze at Madison by Dev's side, arm curled around his leg, and Callie's expression turned contrite. "I'm sorry, honey, I shouldn't swear in front of you. I won't do it again."

"I don't care," Madison declared stoutly.

"Well, I do." Callie rubbed her forehead. "Dev?"

He jerked his gaze her way.

"I asked you some questions?"

"You did?" With some alarm, he realized he hadn't tracked them, had only recognized she wasn't pushing him. It all became too much. "Excuse me." He gently detached Mad from his leg, assuring her he'd be right back, then strode to the bathroom. He thought he would throw up, but there really wasn't anything in his stomach. Instead, he leaned on the sink and stared into the mirror, willing himself to remember just who he was and how he'd got here.

He used to know.

Chapter Nine

"Madison, honey, I'm sorry about this morning." Callie reached for the girl, regretting that Madison had to witness so much.

She climbed right into Callie's lap and looked up, face pale and tight. "Is Scott gone *now?*"

"Not exactly. He's contained." At Madison's puzzled expression, she explained, "He can't talk to anyone right now." This assurance had the girl's thin body relaxing in Callie's hold.

Across the table, a red-eyed Ruth regarded Callie sullenly. "I didn't ask you to visit so you could *attack* Scott."

Callie's anger flared. "Well, surely you didn't ask me to visit so Scott could force Dev to attack me."

"Scott wants to protect us, that's all. He thought you were trying to take over and hurt us."

Callie blinked. That was some explanation and quite frankly she didn't understand it.

"I mean," Ruth added emotionally, "you are taking over. Just not like Scott."

Rather wearily, Callie said, "It wasn't entirely planned, Ruth." Since her words seemed to do little to deflect her sister's anger, Callie stroked Madison's hair. The child, at least, had the sense to keep away from Scott. Unlike Ruth. Callie wondered how Dev was going to take this turn of events. First he had to pull himself together. She was a bit worried about what he was doing in the bathroom.

"I'm glad Scott is *sorta* gone." Madison nestled deeper into Callie arms. "You're better."

She wasn't Scott's replacement, but Callie opted not to argue the point with a seven-year-old. Instead she warned, "Don't go into Ruth's room, sweetie." Then she met her sister's gaze. "You either, Ruth."

"And just how am I supposed to get dressed?" Ruth demanded, and Callie found herself dangerously near laughing at her sister's self-righteousness.

"I will bring your clothes out."

This solution did little to soothe Ruth who continued in a similar vein with, "And where am I supposed to sleep?"

"Ruth, for God's sakes." Callie took a deep breath. If anger and laughter were both so near the surface, she was less in control of her emotions than she wanted to be. She needed to stay calm. An observant and vulnerable child was watching and listening to everything Callie said. "You can sleep in the den like Scott did."

"You've ruined everything," muttered Ruth.

"What was I supposed to do? Let Scott run your lives and just watch him make you nuts? How does he do that anyway? It's creepy, Ruth, his control over you. It's *wrong*."

Ruth stiffened and sniffed back more tears. "I don't know what you're talking about."

"Like—" —*hell*. Callie bit her lip as Madison's gaze went back and forth between the two sisters. Callie had grown up in foster care, and as a child, adults swearing had always made her uneasy. She leaned down to Madison. "I'm not mad at Ruth, sweetie. It's Scott who concerns me."

"He concerns me too," echoed Madison.

Dev emerged from the washroom then, face drawn but composed. He went straight to Madison. "Mad, we adults have to talk."

Something in Callie just melted at the way he made the child his first priority.

Madison eyed Dev and when she spoke, her tone was cajoling. "You said I was mature."

Despite that Dev looked pretty awful, his eyes warmed at Madison's attempt to stay in the kitchen and listen. "You are. You're also seven."

"I can help." She glanced up at Callie. "I know things."

"Oh?" Callie responded in what she hoped was a leading way.

"There have been others."

Callie's stomach dropped. She didn't want the situation to get even more complicated and "others" sounded ominous. Others like Scott, or others like Dev and Ruth? Where were these people now? She was scared to ask.

Dev walked over and lifted Madison off Callie's lap and into his arms. While he carried her to the den, he said, "I know you're bored with TV, and I don't blame you. I promise that after I talk to Callie and Ruth, I'll go outside with you."

"Now that Callie's in charge, do you think I could have some friends?" she asked hopefully.

Dev winced, though whether at the description or at the question, Callie couldn't tell. "In charge"? She didn't know what to make of that. Ruth had talked about her taking over.

"I don't know, Mad," Dev answered rather bleakly after his pause. With that, he turned on the TV, settled Madison in a chair and walked out, closing the door behind him.

He strode over and took a kitchen chair, turned it around and sat on it, his arms resting on its back. It should have been a relaxed pose, but he looked far from relaxed.

Ruth gave a watery sigh of commiseration that he acknowledged with a brief closing of his eyes. Callie waited, unsure what to make of their silent communication. She had so many questions, but how to formulate them so they were useful? How do you ask someone if their "friend" uses mind control on them? Even as a cat shifter, Callie had trouble wrapping her head around the concept.

Dev cleared his throat and stared at the center of the table. "I should speak first? That's what you'd like, Callie?"

The carefully worded question turned her stomach. "What do you mean?"

His eyes cut her way before returning to the table. "I think you know what I mean."

"Well, I don't. I've spent two days in this house, one day with Scott, one without, and I feel pretty much in the dark." She almost said more, almost demanded he tell her what was going on, but Dev seemed to be bracing himself against her words. He held himself rigid, the way she'd seen him with Scott, and instinct told her to tread softly. So she waited for him to speak.

When silence reigned, punctuated only by Ruth biting her nails, Dev gave a short, angry laugh. "You all like to play games. I'd rather you just gave orders. It's more honest."

"Orders," she repeated.

He jerked a nod, mouth set in a tight line.

"I have a request, will that do?" She supposed it wasn't the time to be sarcastic, but this conversation was nerve racking.

"Oh sure," he sneered. She'd seen this expression on him

before and it didn't sit well. It was a last resort for him.

"Please don't go anywhere near Scott. I especially don't want him talking to you or Ruth."

Dev frowned, as if searching for the code behind Callie's words.

Ruth stopped pouting long enough to blurt out, "Oh for God's sakes, Dev. Can't you tell my sister is not one of *them*? Scott just thinks she is." To Callie, she declared, "*I* am not going to listen to you."

"Then what are you going to do?" Callie asked.

"Free him. I have to protect Scott!"

"Protect...?" Callie felt speechless. "*Gah*," she spat, a little too feline for her companions' tastes obviously, as they both were startled by the noise. "Did Scott tell you to protect him, Ruth? How far in the future can he control your actions?"

Ruth just looked back at her blankly. Then, apropos of nothing, or so it seemed to Callie, Ruth declared, "Scott is *very* sensitive."

"Sensitive, huh? Jesus Christ, is that a euphemism for 'complete asshole'?"

"No," protested Ruth, offended now, which just amazed Callie. "How can you talk about Scott that way? He's a wonderful person."

Callie turned to Dev. "What does Ruth mean? Do you think Scott is *sensitive*? I'm pretty sure you don't think Scott is wonderful. Though God knows I could be wrong."

Dev scrubbed his face and gazed straight ahead, looking lost, weary and furious all at once. "What are you doing?" He answered his own question. "Playing games. You've proved you can play, okay?" He leaned forward, so intent, yet never meeting her eyes. "You fooled me, okay? Congratulations." He clenched his fist. "But leave Madison alone. Just let me look after her without your influence. Then I'll do whatever you want. Her brain, it's too young, if you care at all, it's too young to be influenced by you."

"I think I need a decoder ring here." No reaction from Dev and that effort of his, to keep himself in check, was hard to watch. She had to convince him she was on his side. But he wouldn't look at her.

Callie wanted Dev to see her, because it felt like he couldn't stop perceiving her as a Minder. So she moved off her chair and knelt down in front of Dev, forcing him to meet her gaze. He met and held it, flinched but held it, keeping himself there and she understood he was leaving himself open to her. As if she were another Scott. God, what a terrible offer, to do whatever a Scott-type person wanted.

She wanted to reach up and grab his arm, but that was a Scott-type action, so she simply said, "I'm not like Scott. I don't know exactly what *Minders* are, but I'm not one of them. I do not give orders. For example, I cannot tell people to sleep, like Scott did Ruth last night, and then have them sleep." Here she turned to her sister. "Right, Ruth? You slept because he told you to."

"I wanted to sleep," she replied immediately. "I always want to sleep." Her eyes were bright and empty. "We need to free Scott, Callie."

"No." Callie turned back to watch for Dev's reaction to this. He was clutching the back of the chair now. She didn't think he could get more tense, and she had the impression that fury thrummed through him. For a moment she thought he wouldn't speak.

He forced out those words again, making Callie's stomach roil. "You fooled me, okay?"

"For fuck's sake, Dev, you already said that." Ruth stood suddenly, and Callie feared she would have to physically restrain her sister to keep her away from Scott. Instead, Ruth approached Dev, contempt on her pretty face. Callie didn't remember Ruth being contemptuous. There'd been some personality changes here, she knew that, but this was more than she'd bargained for. "You're becoming a zombie, Dev."

"Scott doesn't make zombies." One of those canned responses that Callie had to assume originally came from Scott, as Dev's speech was wooden and not particularly comprehensible, at least to Callie.

"Ruth," Callie said slowly. "Why are you talking about zombies?" What an awful word. She hated it.

"Dev is Scott's, but Scott promised I wouldn't be his as long as I was good and stayed healthy." A pause while Ruth's expression became determined. "Which I have. I was good."

"*What* are you talking about?" demanded Callie, seriously floundering. She wanted answers, not more gibberish.

Dev was wiping his eyes now, which Callie found a little heartbreaking. She longed to hold him. Puma even wanted to hold him. When was the last time her two halves had been in sync? But she held back, scared to startle him.

He gazed at Callie again, that unfocused look, and rasped the words out. "You fooled me, okay?"

And she couldn't help it. She knew he didn't like touch. She knew Scott had messed with him, and he was scared she was messing with him. But everything in Callie told her to rise up and place two hands on Dev, on his arms.

He flinched, sucking in air, but he didn't fight it. She very slowly pulled him down to the floor with her, because the chairs just got in the way and she'd never been a great one for furniture. Now that they were connected, she rubbed his shoulder, trying to soothe him with her touch.

"I did not fool you, Dev."

He moved, abruptly, grabbing her, both her arms in his grip, his embrace a mirror of hers, much less gentle but not bruising. He spoke through clenched teeth. "What the fuck is going on here?"

"That's what I'm trying to figure out. You have to help me." She moved her hand to rub the side of his neck, and they were both breathing hard, Dev for his own terrible reasons, and Callie because she found the sensation of being touched by Dev so intense.

"What are you?" he demanded. "Why can you ignore Scott?"

She had to answer the question. To evade would raise all Dev's suspicions to too high a pitch. And yet, what an answer. "I'm a cougar." At his what-the-fuck expression, she amended, "Sometimes."

"A cougar likes sex, Callie!"

"What?" Puma didn't like sex at all. Mostly because there were no fellow cat shifters to have sex with. But still.

He gave her a sharp shake. "You make no fucking sense."

"Well, neither do you." It sounded childish, she knew, but he looked so furious, when he was the one who came out with cryptic, repetitive phrases.

God, what a pair the two of them made.

Then his anger seemed to bank, sat there in his eyes, focusing on her as he made a decision.

"What?" she asked again.

His hands skimmed up her arms, to her shoulders, neck, jaw, cheeks. Holding her face, he tilted her head to the right as if examining a strange new phenomenon. One hand slid back to anchor in her hair and she shivered, feeling awkward and

114

exhilarated by his attention, though this was neither the time nor place.

His mouth came down on hers.

She stiffened right up, not sure how to respond as he entered her, tongue sweeping into her mouth, demanding...demanding what? He groaned, his hand fisting her hair and tilting her head back as he rose on his knees above her, forcing her to lean back in their embrace. Her brain couldn't catch up as his thumb stroked the side of her neck and his kiss gentled while he explored her mouth and coaxed her tongue to respond. She relaxed a little. Though she usually didn't like kissing, she liked Dev and this was so *unexpected.*

"Why the hell are you two making out?" Ruth stood over them, sounding furious.

Dev tamped down on the kiss, withdrawing, though he caught her bottom lip between his teeth before he let go, his gaze on hers, molten, no longer angry, but something just as intense.

"You're *not* a cougar," he repeated, "not that you're old enough anyway. God, who calls themselves cougars anyway?" This last question seemed to be muttered to himself.

"Puma then," said Callie in an attempt to clarify. For him to understand, she'd have to shift before his eyes, but he might not want to understand.

"No one calls themselves cougars." Dev seemed stuck on this point.

"Well there aren't very many of us." Callie was trying not to get offended. "I'm probably the first you've met."

"Callie," said Ruth impatiently, "has this *thing* for big cats. She used to watch videos all the time and sometimes pretended she was one, prowl around the house. Very odd."

Dev gave his head a hard shake, released his hold on Callie, and rose. She'd liked his hands on her, even his mouth on her, unexpected as it had been. Their gazes locked, she brought fingers to her hot lips and Dev watched her, eyes smoldering. Then he wrenched his gaze away and focused on her sister.

"Uh, Ruth, an obsession with big cats sounds pretty benign as things go. And you *know* how fucked things can get." He scrubbed his face, then stood, appearing less edgy than he had ten minutes ago.

Ruth grabbed Dev and he allowed it, though Callie could see he wanted Ruth to release him. "We need to free Scott, Dev. You of all people understand we do. You're loyal, Dev, I know it."

Callie scrambled to her feet.

"Do you want to go to him now, Ruth? Do you really?" Dev asked. A look of distaste passed over her features as she nodded. "I don't think you do. And I, I just *can't*. I need a break."

"It's our duty."

"Says who?" demanded Callie.

"It just *is*." Ruth frowned. "You have to take the good with the bad."

God, did Scott like these little homilies? Was he the source of them? "Do you think Scott controls you, Ruth?" Callie asked softly.

"No. Not me." Ruth raised her palm and slashed it through the air to emphasize her point. Then she added, ill at ease, "Dev, maybe. But only because Scott cares."

"Uh-huh. Scott is hurting you both. I can see it," said Callie.

Ruth scoffed, but she still hadn't moved away from the kitchen, had yet to try to save Scott despite all her talk. Callie thought that ultimately Ruth didn't want to. So maybe this mind control was a bit hit and miss. Or maybe Scott wasn't all that good. Or maybe...well, who the fuck knows. This was all so new to her.

"Ruth, I think you wanted me to come visit to get you away from Scott, even if he's so messed with your head you can't admit it. Remember that email you sent me? You wrote that Scott made you nervous."

Ruth just shrugged off Callie's comments irritably.

"Why not you, Callie?" Dev stared down at the table, avoiding her gaze again, his voice a bare murmur. "Why can't he influence you?"

"I don't know," Callie admitted. "He speaks to me as if he expects me to do what he wants. So I did, sometimes, just to go along and try to understand what was going on."

"You never felt you *should*?" Ruth was quite struck by Callie shaking her head. "But Scott always has the best ideas."

Callie sighed. "How long have you known Scott, Dev?"

"I don't know. Years. Or maybe he told me years." He grimaced. "I can't keep things straight, you see."

She wanted to lean into him, but it would have been an awkward action and his body language, despite that kiss, had returned to *don't touch me*. His arms were crossed, his shoulders stiff.

"I've got to talk to Scott." Callie recoiled from the idea; she found the way he used words abhorrent. Yet in the end, he might be a better source of information than either Ruth or Dev. "What are you two going to do?"

"I need to get outside." Dev jabbed a thumb backwards

towards the den where Madison sat. "Poor Mad needs an outing too."

"Will you leave? Now that I've tied up Scott?" asked Callie. Maybe he'd run. She might, if she were in his shoes. The idea of not seeing Dev filled her with dismay, even if she wanted him to get away from Scott. Maybe she could track Dev later. Trey might help her. He had unusual resources. All this ran through her mind while Dev was slowly shaking his head.

"I don't think I can," he muttered, before turning away and going into the den.

"Why can't he leave?" Callie asked Ruth. "Can you?"

"This is our house. We never leave it." That slight lack of inflection indicated these were Scott's words. Okay, so Scott could create some long-term behavior. Perhaps he'd worked harder on this stay-at-the-house behavior than that of Dev and Ruth protecting Scott. Perhaps Scott hadn't thought he'd ever need to be protected, given his powers. He certainly hadn't counted on a puma's arrival, Callie thought a little grimly.

"I'm going upstairs." Callie took in a fortifying breath and stalked down the hall.

Scott would be waiting for her, but what he would say, she couldn't begin to guess.

Chapter Ten

Callie pushed the door open, wincing at the sight of Scott handcuffed to the bed. He'd pulled himself up into a ball, and the position made him look very young.

He wasn't even Ruth's age. Rather plain looking, usually. Now a bruise was forming on his temple, and his eyes were blazing at her. It wasn't simply anger, though the anger was there. He was definitely frightened. Cornered.

Well, if she were clamped to a bed, she'd feel cornered too. The puma in her hated being restrained. But Scott was not a shifter, he was something else entirely.

He raised his chin, defiant in his helplessness. "You think you can take over. Maybe you're right. I've never claimed to be one of the strongest." He swallowed after that admission. "If you were really strong you sure as hell wouldn't need to handcuff me." He rattled his right hand for effect.

"No?" Was she supposed to feel challenged by that statement?

At that apparently feeble response, Scott cast her a look of contempt. "Don't you take some pride in your words?"

"Not usually, if you must know."

He blinked, momentarily thrown off stride by her response. Then he marshaled his contempt again. "Max and Eleanor will come, and they will ruin you all."

Cheery stuff, thought Callie, noting the slight tremor in Scott's voice. "Max? Eleanor?" she asked so he would elaborate.

"I hope you're playing dumb, because Eleanor is going to shred you. She doesn't take kindly to interlopers." Callie's bafflement must have shown, because Scott added, "Most pod leaders don't. You can't pretend not to know *that*."

"I don't even know why Ruth had handcuffs in her room, and I'm not sure I want to know. Nor have I heard of pod leaders. So I don't know about shredding either." She pulled up the chair and sat. Not too close. While Scott's strength wasn't physical, it was best to be cautious. Besides, she didn't feel like breaking her knuckles on his head again. His fresh bruise gave her a pang of regret she'd rather not re-experience, and her hand still throbbed from that punch she'd landed.

"So, Scott, tell me what a pod leader is."

"You think you're fucking funny." He gave a snort of disgust. "If you gave a shit about your sister, you'd have been more careful and checked out the local pod first, asked permission." Here he glared again, eyes bright with rage. "You don't care about Ruth, do you?"

"I care," Callie answered shortly. "But that's not what we're going to discuss right now, okay?"

He sneered in response and she suppressed a sigh. She wasn't entirely sure how you made someone talk when they didn't want to. Well, unless you were a Minder. She'd have to hope that Scott did want to talk, despite his situation.

She'd ask nicely. "I'd like you to explain what you mean by 'local pod'. That wouldn't happen to be a group of Minders you're associated with, would it? A pack of wolves, a murder of crows...and a pod of Minders?"

Scott continued to curl his lip at her, but the way his body folded in on itself showed he felt wounded.

She leaned forward, holding his gaze, and spoke very clearly. "I don't know what the fuck you're talking about half the time. It's like some secret-society code that you believe I understand. But I do not. You are the first person I have ever met who could use this mind control, or whatever you want to call it, on others."

He actually rolled his eyes.

"You think I'm lying?"

He jerked his head in a nod.

"I'm not. If you insist in believing I am, then humor me. Explain to me exactly what a Minder is, Scott, and what he does. What *you* do."

"Please." The scoffing tone would have been more effective if his voice hadn't quavered slightly.

"I'm not a Minder."

He looked down to examine the metal braceleting his wrist. His chest moved in and out quickly, as he tried to contain his panic. Somehow, Callie should have taken more satisfaction at putting this fear into him, given how she despised the way he'd controlled Ruth and Dev.

Instead, she felt a little sick about their present relationship of prisoner and captor. In truth, Scott was about to become a problem she didn't want to deal with—too dangerous to set free and yet the burden of imprisoning him weighed heavily on her.

She realized he was muttering to himself and paid attention as he repeated, "Don't believe, don't believe, she can make you believe."

"I can*not*." She enunciated the two words, as if precise diction would convince him. "I've told you, I'm not a Minder."

While she had some desire to share her shifter status with a fellow freak, she opted not to tell him she was a cat. Puma pitied Scott, even wanted to calm the panicked boy, but ultimately didn't trust the young male. Despite all Callie's problems with her other half, she didn't discard Puma's instincts when it came to people.

He lifted his head, only to drop it back on the headboard and shut his eyes as he spoke to the ceiling. "A Minder, boys and girls, is a *freak*"—she startled at his use of that same word—"of nature who can speak words and make them someone else's thoughts."

"All right." That had been what she'd thought, but to have it so baldly stated... "So, for example, you tell Ruth to sleep calmly and deeply, and she does."

He didn't answer right away and then rather listlessly said, "I've taken good care of Ruth."

"Why?"

"Why what?"

"Why would you take good care of my sister?"

"Are you really sisters?"

"I'm the one asking the questions here."

"Or what? You'll knock me out? Tie me up? Oh wait, you already did that." He jerked his handcuffed arm, shaking the bed. "The only reason I'm talking to you is on the off-chance you're serious and you don't know about Eleanor. Ruth and Dev used to belong to her, till I got them out. If they go back to her, she will use and discard them, and they might as well be dead. Madison will go to Max and he's just as bad. They're our pod's leader and enforcer." Scott's mouth twisted.

"That's quite a dramatic statement, Scott."

He shrugged. "I'm a drama queen, that's me. However,

there are worse than me."

"Okay, let me get this straight. There are people, Minders, worse than you?"

"Yes." He actually looked hurt, which just made Callie angry.

"Do you understand how much you've been fucking with Dev's mind? He scrambles to keep his thoughts together. He's close to the edge, anyone with eyes can see it."

Scott licked his lips and for the first time sounded a little desperate, as though he cared what Callie thought. "I only push Dev when I have to. The problem is he's a fighter. He doesn't give way easily. We knew that going in."

"Fighter? Going in? Can you translate?"

"Dev resists suggestion at every turn. Some people are like that. With anyone else but me, they wouldn't last long. But I care." He gave a soundless laugh, probably at the disbelief on Callie's face. "Ruth, by the way, isn't a resister. That's why Eleanor had her so long."

Callie winced at the idea of some woman "having" Ruth as a type of possession.

"Yeah," said Scott, nodding, expression now earnest. "That's why I wanted to rescue Ruth. Dev did too."

She frowned. "They're here. You're not saving them."

"You don't know what you're talking about."

She rolled her eyes.

"Okay, yes, Dev's struggling. I'll admit that."

"Why wouldn't you let Dev go, if what you're doing is so bad for him? If you can see it. You shouldn't pretend you care about Dev. It's a farce."

At this, Scott took affront. "I *saved* Dev."

"God, from what?" Callie stood up, having a hard time imagining a worse nightmare for Dev.

"Eleanor." Scott shook the bed again, yanking with his handcuffs. "You ask Dev about Eleanor. You say the name 'Eleanor' to Dev and see how he reacts."

She stared at her captive, his gray gaze dark and stormy. His pale face made even paler by his new powerlessness.

"Okay, let's set aside Eleanor for a moment." She wondered if this bogeywoman actually existed. Real or not, she had to play it safe and assume yes. "I have another question. Ruth keeps talking about protecting and saving *you*." Callie couldn't help but think there was a lot of bullshit talk about saving going round here. "And yet, unlike the sleeping she did last night, she does not act in any way to save or protect you. She only talks about it."

Scott looked embarrassed. "I didn't do a good job."

"Of what?"

"Convincing her to protect me. Mostly, I didn't think she would need to. It was all about me rescuing her, you see." He sounded defensive, as if Callie was questioning his abilities. "Also Ruth probably doesn't want to, save me, that is. Whereas, she wants to sleep." He shrugged. "I'm not good at seeding longer-term actions unless they're in line with what the person wants."

"So the effect of your words depends in part on how much a person wants to do them?"

He regarded her warily. "Of course."

"Then why doesn't Dev leave this house?"

Scott smiled, a slightly secretive expression. "I think you won't believe me. *He doesn't want to.*"

"You're right, I don't believe you."

"You understand nothing and you're going to ruin everyone's life here, Callie. Everyone's." His voice was rising and Callie could swear he believed himself.

"Because of Max, the evil pod leader."

"*Eleanor* is the pod leader, Max the enforcer. Are you stupid, or just goading me?"

"I haven't taken Minder 101 yet, Scott."

"If you want a crash course, wait around until Max appears. Watch and learn while everyone suffers. Or *dies*," he added dramatically.

Callie rubbed her forehead, both aggravated and alarmed by Scott's dire tone. "What do you predict will happen?"

"He'll take control."

Callie almost said, *Not of me*, but chose to remain silent. She didn't do bravado, even in front of someone chained to a bed.

"You may not be immune to Max." Scott swiped his face with his hand, and the way he bent over, exposing his neck, made him look young and helpless, made him appeal to the puma in her who liked to protect those she met who needed protection. Scott stank of fear and it was the only thing that stopped her from lashing out at him.

"I think I'll be okay," she said quietly.

"Even if you are"—he raised his face—"he'll kill you for being immune, and then convince everyone around him that he didn't. He's that powerful. He has his local police in the palm of his hand."

"It sounds quite hopeless."

Scott didn't react, though his confusion at her dry tone came through clearly. He actually expected her to become panicked by these pronouncements.

"Do you think I'm stupid, Scott?"

He flinched, just slightly, so she supposed there'd been threat in her voice. She hadn't meant to put it there, but he was making her angry.

"No, I don't," he said carefully.

"Then why tell me all this? Why prepare me for my own bloodletting? Just let Max the enforcer waltz in here and either enslave or kill me. Then you can get back to your happy little life with Dev and Ruth and Madison under your control."

"Eleanor is going to be extremely *unhappy* with me for having *lost* control. In her eyes, I'll have proven I'm weak. Max will be allowed..." His voice trailed off.

"Allowed to do what?"

"You don't want to know."

"You're quite wrong. I do want to know." She gestured for him to continue.

Scott examined his handcuff, then spoke to it. "Weak Minders are considered a liability. They can expose the pod. At the very least I will be punished."

She frowned, wondering at his potential punishment, but before she could ask, he continued, "I don't want to be hurt. I don't want Dev and Ruth and Madison to return to Eleanor and Max, for they will take them back and destroy them."

It was hard not to think of this as hyperbole, even if the boy seemed incredibly earnest. Hysteria and earnestness, quite a strange combination. Callie let out a long sigh. "What do you want, Scott?"

"Let me go," he entreated, eyes pleading, and Callie was oddly tempted. She wondered idly if that was his ability working on her at a low level, or if she simply had a soft spot for a fellow freak. "I'll leave the house, go back to the pod, Eleanor won't know anything about you. She'll have no reason to think something has gone wrong at this house."

"You must know I can't do that. I simply can't trust you." Callie decided it was unwise to say out loud that Scott, with his powers, might be able to convince someone to do her harm. He hadn't succeeded in making Dev punch her, but another person might be more malleable. Apart from that, Scott shouldn't be able to harm normals the way he'd been doing, and she could not allow it to continue. She'd certainly stopped other freaks from harming the world at large. God knows she had led werecougars to their deaths.

She flinched from that last thought, found she didn't want to bring someone in to be killed again, even if Scott needed to be contained. "I can't let you go, Scott."

He nodded, having expected her answer, and licked his lips. "If you can't do that, there's another thing I would ask of you. If you can do it."

"And that is?"

"I want you to kill Eleanor."

She blinked in surprise, then stared into his eyes, wishing they could tell her what to believe of this strange young Minder who foretold of death and punishment. Was he deranged? Was he a liar?

To her horror, Callie realized she believed him, believed he wanted her to kill Eleanor, that is. Obviously, she needed a break from this conversation.

"I'll be right back."

She left the room, feeling a palpable sense of relief as she shut the door and leaned against it. Slowly, she made her way downstairs only to be accosted by Ruth who gripped her arm and gazed at her imploringly. "How is Scott? Did you hurt him?"

Callie had this terrible desire to joke that she'd ripped Scott's throat out, which wasn't funny even if it were a joke that Ruth would get.

"Well." God, how to sum up Scott and his state of affairs? "He's a little stressed. So am I. He should have something to eat and drink, I think."

"Oh, right. Food." Ruth paused, brow creasing. "But Dev's not here."

Something snapped in Callie. "For fuck's sake, Ruth, can you not get Scott some juice and a sandwich? Is that such a challenge?"

"Yes." Ruth glared. "It's just that, I dunno, I just *know* that's Dev's job. I'm *used* to it. It's the *routine.*"

"Okay, sorry." Callie held up both hands in surrender. This wasn't simply Ruth being lazy, this was Ruth who'd been living with a Minder for months apparently. "I know things have been very structured here for a while, but you need to be flexible now. And we need to figure out what is going on." As Ruth pulled bread and cheese out of the fridge, Callie asked, "You realize things haven't been right in this house, eh, Ruth? That Scott's been controlling you?"

"I wanted him to." Said with little inflection.

"Or does he want you to believe you want him to?"

Ruth straightened, set down the food and slammed the flat of her hand on the counter. "I don't care. Honest to God, I don't care."

"Okay." Enough of that topic. Ruth angrily put together a sandwich, scraping butter over the bread, mashing it a bit. Callie grabbed some food and drink for herself while Ruth prepared Scott's snack. When she was done, Callie braced herself to ask her sister, "Who is Eleanor?"

"Who?" She had a distracted air, but Ruth wasn't distressed.

"Eleanor." Callie expected more of a reaction after Scott's somewhat hysterical description of the pod leader. Going by Ruth's expression, she didn't even recognize the name.

"I don't know." Ruth shoved the sandwich at Callie who reached for a plastic plate.

Callie leaned a hip against the counter. "Where were you before you met Scott?"

At that, Ruth's eyes clouded over, then she gave a quick shake of her head. "I don't want to think about it."

Callie bit her lip, wondering if she should ask more. Or perhaps first ask Dev. "Where's Dev?"

"He took Madison outside. She wanted to go for a bike ride."

"All right. I'll take the sandwich up to Scott."

Ruth didn't argue, which made Callie suspect she didn't actually want to be in Scott's presence, but still Callie warned, "Don't go near Scott, okay?"

"Yeah, yeah. I heard you before." Ruth let out a long breath. "I'm feeling more comfortable now. With what you've done. Like maybe...maybe I needed to stay away from Scott a little. See, usually he comes and goes quickly, doesn't stay here this long. You changed that."

"I certainly changed something," Callie agreed and with that she carried food and drink up to Scott.

He was gazing at her as she shouldered the door open, his body still balled up against the headboard.

"Hungry?" Callie asked.

"I skipped breakfast."

"Oh, that's right. Dev was supposed to make pancakes and

we got distracted and only the bacon got fried." She passed Scott the juice first, which he took in his free hand. She briefly wondered if he'd throw the drink at her in a fit of pique, but he simply brought it to his mouth and gulped it down before handing back the empty glass. Well, she'd made a point of bringing up a plastic glass so he couldn't brain her with it or hurt himself with any potential shards. She didn't think he really wanted to do himself harm, but she couldn't tell for sure. Especially with his apparent fear of these other Minders.

She placed the glass on the dresser and turned back. "So tell me, what's with Dev doing all the cooking and food stuff?"

"He likes to cook."

"All the time?"

"Enough that he doesn't resist my suggestion he keep everyone well fed. He needs to keep busy. He's an active kind of guy."

"I see. So you're doing him a favor, really, getting him to make you meals."

"I only visit. It's the others he feeds." Scott paused, hungry eyes on the plate. "Do I get my sandwich?"

"Ruth made it."

"It'll be shit, then."

"It's edible." She handed him the plastic plate and he picked up the sandwich in both hands and began eating hungrily. It wasn't going to be enough. He was a young man. They ate a lot. Not as much as shifters of course, but more than this meager sandwich.

"Tell me why Dev doesn't want to leave this house," Callie said abruptly when he was almost done eating.

He swallowed his bite. "Ask him yourself."

"I will. But asking Dev questions can be painful. Hurtful to him, I think. So I need to do it sparingly, choose my questions with care."

"There are much worse ways in which Dev can be hurt."

"Yes, yes, I've picked that up. Just answer me."

"Dev wants to be with me." Scott wiped his mouth after his last bite. There was something triumphant in the statement.

"I don't think so," Callie said slowly. "Or he would have come to this room."

Here, Scott's gaze slid away. "I've miscalculated," he admitted. Then he hung his head while he laughed a little. "You know, it is a bitter, strange, yet enormous relief to be talking to you. Or it is when I believe you aren't another Minder toying with me."

"I'm not a Minder." It seemed like she couldn't say that enough today. "You miscalculated...?"

He stared at his handcuff. "I thought Dev could withstand a couple of years under my sway." Scott gripped his hands together, wringing them. "You think he's close to cracking?"

"Come on. You know it."

"Dev thought he could do it, you know."

"What?"

"He agreed. He was always a do-gooder, the protective kind. That's how he met the others, of course."

"Explain, Scott."

"We were going to rescue people, Dev and I, once he realized what Eleanor was. We did a few. Ruth was a junkie, getting used in every way possible by Max and Eleanor."

Callie felt sick and she hoped Scott was just trying to freak her out about Ruth, that this wasn't true. "Don't fuck with me, Scott. I have a lousy temper."

Scott was on a roll. "Max didn't know what to do with Madison. She was a little girl who cried all the time and wasn't very useful. Helen was hired out as a prostitute by Eleanor. Ian slit his wrists but got found in time."

"I think you're making this up. I think *you* are toying with me. I think you don't know how not to toy with people."

"*I* think you don't understand what you've walked into. I just hope to God you can handle Max because he'll arrive here first." With that, Scott turned over, put his back to Callie and stared out the window. "If you can't beat Max, I'm going to slit my own wrists."

Either Scott was a very good actor, or he believed what he said. Callie was too pissed by his histrionics to figure it out. She went downstairs to wait for Dev's return. While Dev wouldn't welcome it, she desperately needed to ask him some more questions.

Chapter Eleven

Callie didn't talk to Dev till the end of the day. He avoided her, pretty much using Madison as a shield, intentionally or no, while he showered attention on the child. There was a lightness to him, as if the shadow of Scott's presence had lessened. Even if Scott was directly upstairs. Callie found she was ready to give Dev a few hours of peace and herself a few hours of mental preparation—she wasn't exactly used to being in charge of a Minder—before they sat down and figured out how to get out of this mess they found themselves in, and what they were actually going to do about their prisoner.

Callie went in and out of Scott's room, delivering more food and drink, and dealing with the slight awkwardness of Scott using the toilet. There were more dire warnings and he made the occasional attempt to "push" her. She was getting the hang of some of the lingo. The people a Minder controlled were sometimes called zombies, but Scott disliked that term. One of the very few things, perhaps, that Callie and Scott had in common.

"They're actually my friends," he told her with a kind of awful earnestness. "I'm as careful as I can be with them." Callie didn't bother to voice her "yeah, right" reaction to that declaration.

Ruth set up her bedding on the couch in the den and

crawled into bed early. Scott, too, slept shortly after the sun set. The day's events had exhausted them all. When Callie left the boy sleeping, Dev was standing at the threshold of his room, arms crossed, evidently waiting for her, a weariness now dragging down his expression.

He didn't want to talk, that's what his body language said, but he gestured for her to enter, and she walked past him.

As she did, she became acutely aware of him, his unique scent, the breaths he took, the curve of his well-muscled shoulders. He'd kissed her and with everything that had happened since then, she'd almost, well, forgotten wasn't the right word—given that she'd occasionally touched her lips during the rest of the day—but she had set the kiss aside.

He had surprised her, given his distinct distaste for touch, and yet there had been some kind of desire there—she thought. She wasn't an expert on these matters by any means.

"How is Scott?" Dev's question jolted her back to the problem at hand and she turned towards him.

"Tired, actually. He's sleeping."

"How are you keeping him in the room?"

"I handcuffed him to the bed."

He lifted his eyebrows in surprise. "Where the hell did you get handcuffs?"

"I didn't. Ruth had them. God knows why and I haven't had the strength to ask her. She's resented the questions I have asked, and it seemed less important to find out about handcuffs than her history with Scott."

"What are you going to do?"

"What are *you* going to do?" She knew the echo sounded unsophisticated, but she wanted to know what was on his mind, if he planned anything.

He scrubbed his face. "Nothing."

"Nothing? Why not leave? Now that Scott can't talk to you, you can escape. Isn't that what you want?" She couldn't imagine Dev wanting to be under Scott's control, under anyone's control.

Dev looked a little ill. "I can't." At her confusion, he added, "I can't leave Scott."

"You don't even talk about rescuing him, like Ruth, so why can't you leave him?"

"I owe him," he said listlessly.

"That's Scott talking."

Dev shrugged. "Could be. Doesn't matter."

"It sure as hell *matters*, Dev."

That seemed to ignite something in him, and he took two long strides towards her, gripped her shoulders. "I can't leave Scott. *I owe him.*"

"You don't. He's...he's..." It was hard to say it directly to Dev whose dark eyes looked so intently at Callie. But she had to. "He's abused you, Dev."

Instead of replying, or even responding to her statement, his gaze dropped to her mouth. His hand slid over her shoulder, across to her neck; fingers forked up into her hair and made a fist to anchor her head so she couldn't move. His mouth was a mere breath from hers.

"I'm going to kiss you, Callie." He watched for her reaction and she didn't know if she was supposed to give a verbal yes, or not. He must have seen something to encourage him. She thought he would kiss like before: sudden, deep, all his for the taking.

His lips brushed hers and before she could protest his leaving, he returned, caught her lower lip between his gentle teeth, scraped it lightly. Like the end of this morning's kiss, but this was a beginning. A noise rose from her throat, in question, in desire, and with the fist that held her hair in his grip, he angled her head.

"God," he said, a guttural sound, before his mouth covered hers, forcing her mouth open, stroking her tongue with his. He tasted of mint and chocolate and Dev; and she tried to welcome him though all she could do was accept as he devoured her. She'd been kissed before and hadn't much liked it, hadn't liked the invasion. Dev was different, demanding, yes, but focused on her. His large hand splayed across her back, between her shoulder blades, and pushed her flush against him so they had full-body contact. The flood of sensation, from his talented mouth—she had never felt so thoroughly kissed, his tongue demanding hers to dance, then withdrawing to explore her lips before delving in again—to the warmth of his body pressed against hers.

She actually went weak in the knees.

As she sank against him, he cupped the back of her head, holding her in that kiss, while the other arm wrapped around her waist, anchoring her to him. He slid his hand under her T-shirt and clasped her ribs, his palm and fingers warm against her skin.

His tongue released hers, and he retreated to nibble her lips. He kissed across her jawline and descended to her neck where he sucked at the sensitive skin there. Her throat vibrated, half-groan, half-purr, all pleasure. As he kissed across her collarbone, he said, "Callie, Callie. I want us to make love."

He pulled back sharply then, as if to give himself a shake, and she reached for him, hands on his shoulders, scared he would go away. She couldn't stand it, couldn't take being released by him now.

He eyed her while he raised his hands to rest upon hers. For a terrible moment, she feared he was going to remove her hold on him, return to that "don't touch" manner he sometimes projected. Instead, he caressed the backs of her hands, feather-soft strokes of his fingertips over her knuckles, between her knuckles and, most sensitively, between her fingers. She trembled in reaction, amazed that her hands could react to his touch so. A warmth gathered in her belly.

He did lift her hands off, but linked fingers with his and brought their arms down together, pulling her up against him again. Perhaps he too craved touch despite his... She bit her lip.

"What, Callie?"

"Earlier you said you weren't interested in sex."

He stiffened and she closed her eyes, wishing the thought hadn't flitted through her mind, wishing she could have lied or at least fobbed him off with a "nothing", though it was important to her that she be honest with Dev.

She rested her face against the crook of his neck and willed him not to push her away after her reminder. When she kissed him, he shuddered. They were soft, almost chaste kisses, not like his that had ravaged her neck.

He brought her arms behind her, clasped both wrists in one large hand, while with his other, he pressed a palm against the small of her back. Her belly felt him hard against her. Aroused.

That made her smile into his neck.

"Look at me," he demanded, so she tilted her head back to meet his gaze. "You like that, that you've made me hard, that you've made me want you?"

"Yes." She struggled a little, which resulted in her writhing against him, but he didn't release her arms. Lifting his free hand to her face, he held her gaze to his, palm on her cheek.

With the pad of his thumb, he traced the bone just under her eye, traced her cheekbone, then ran that thumb over her lips.

"You're beautiful."

It made her breathe faster, these words, these intense caresses, this attention. He trailed fingers down her neck to the swell of her breast. He was watching her very carefully as he lightly palmed her breast and her sensitive nipple began to ache.

"Dev?" She wasn't sure what she was asking.

"Hmmm?" His mouth dipped to her neck, teeth scraping the soft skin, then soothing it with a kiss. And again. His hand slipped under the hem of her T-shirt, and rose to catch her nipple between thumb and finger, rolling the nub. "Do you like that?" he murmured as he kissed her throat.

She arched against him and he swallowed her "yes", his mouth taking hers in a punishing kiss.

Her knees gave out this time, but he caught her, finally releasing her arms, though not her mouth, as he lifted her and she wrapped herself around him. He brought her to the bed.

She tried to contain her disappointment as he set her down on the mattress. He yanked off her shirt, then his, her shorts then his, all in short order. It had been a revelation, this kind of foreplay, but now he was ready to fuck.

He crawled over her and for a moment she thought he was going to move up so he'd fuck her mouth, but he reached back and pulled her up so they were face to face again, her under him. He'd wanted to make love, she remembered, and that reassured her.

"You make me feel, Callie." The words seemed almost to be dragged from him and she touched his face, roughened because he hadn't shaved.

"I think you're beautiful too, Dev." She wanted to offer him something of her feelings, though that barely described her real emotions. Tentatively she ran a hand through his short hair, which was surprisingly soft to touch.

"Are you scared to touch me, Callie?"

"No." The question caught her off guard, and it must have shown.

"You prefer that I touch you?" He skimmed a hand down her side and across her stomach. Her underside. It made her feel vulnerable and he seemed to notice, because he crossed his palm back and forth across her soft belly until she relaxed into the touch. "Tell me what you like," he urged.

She didn't know. He traced some ribs, but he didn't release her gaze so she said, "I like you."

He smiled then, so pleased, the smile wider than she'd observed before, like she was seeing a new Dev.

"I like everything you do. You make me feel so warm. Inside."

His slightly bemused expression made her add, "Is that wrong to say?"

"No," he said immediately. "Nothing is wrong to say." He sat back and she feared he was retreating, giving up on them making love. Perhaps because he thought she didn't like to touch him? That wasn't it, wasn't it at all. She was just so unsure, but she began to rise, to follow him.

He came back, pushing her down, lying atop her, that full-body contact she craved, though he took some of the weight with his elbows. He kissed her deeply, a kind of reassurance, then broke away and held her shoulders. "Stay here."

Again he sat up. Instead of backing away, he pulled up both her legs, ran palms over her thighs, front and back. Then calves were caressed before he wrapped his hands around her ankles to place her feet down near her butt, knees pointed up. She frowned at him and he smiled, resting hands on her knees. He pushed them apart, making her legs drop open.

She felt completely exposed and very, very wet.

"You, Callie, are going to tell me if at any time you feel *uncomfortable*, okay?"

Her chest rose and fell as he placed the heel of his palm on her pubis and rubbed lightly. Surprised, realizing she was completely ready, she arched up to push against his hand. "Dev, I want you inside me."

He didn't answer, but instead traced the folds surrounding her pussy. She was slick with her own juices and it seemed to make him smile.

He laid his face against her belly, his rough cheek scraping her skin. He slid one finger into her and her bones began to melt. "I'd like that too, Callie." His finger slid out, back in and she thrashed, her throat vibrating, even as she tried to recall what he could like. "But I can't be inside you."

"Why *not*?" she asked in total bafflement. No guy had ever balked at this point in the game.

"I have no condoms." There was regret in his voice, even as he continued to touch her so intimately.

She gripped the sheet in order not to arch off the bed, but he didn't stop. In fact, he slid two fingers in which made it both better and worse, because she wanted more.

"Doesn't matter," she panted. "I..." *can't get or give disease.* Explaining that shifting to cat and back to human got rid of all diseases, that it healed her, was too complicated for the here and now. He hadn't exactly accepted her statement that she was a cougar, and besides her brain was too muddled to explain it properly. "I'm clean."

"I'll make you come, Callie, don't worry about that." Again he rubbed his cheek against her belly. Then his hand crept up to touch her nipple and she thought she was going to explode. "I'm clean too, but I won't risk pregnancy."

She couldn't think. He rolled the nipple, just this side of painful, and sank those two fingers deep, held them there as his thumb rubbed against her clit.

She couldn't breathe, her chest tightened and tightened, and she was shaking.

"Callie, Callie," he murmured as if she were everything in the world to him. He kissed her belly.

"God!" She shattered, out of nowhere she seemed to crash into a sharp white bliss that rocked her body, and for a moment she wasn't quite there...

When she floated back, languor was invading her body and Dev was sucking her breast, his two fingers still impaled in her, like they belonged there.

It was an effort to lift her eyelids. But she wanted him. "My tubes are tied."

He lifted his head and stared at her, clearly doubtful.

"I don't lie, Dev, and I wouldn't lie about this."

"Be careful. You may convince me. You don't know"—he swallowed, perhaps because his voice sounded so rough—"how long it has been, how much I want to be inside you."

She moved down a little to position herself so that his cock was at her entrance.

He closed his eyes and she had the impression he was about to make some kind of heroic effort to withdraw.

"Please don't leave me like this, Dev. Please trust me when I say you can't make me pregnant."

His eyes grew even darker. "Callie," he warned, but it

wasn't just a warning it was a promise, and she said, "*Yes.*" He thrust into her, filling her, stretching her, and she gasped at the suddenness of it. He didn't move then, which shocked her even more. He stayed motionless, trembling slightly with the effort as she adjusted to his presence. He cupped her head in both hands, a strangely tender embrace, and forced her to look at him.

"Okay, Callie?"

That sensation was building again and suddenly everything felt like brand-new territory, overwhelming, and yet something she could not do without. "Don't leave me."

"I'm not going anywhere, babe."

She smiled at his endearment and he took it as encouragement, because he began to move.

"Oh my God," she said. He moved within her and she arched into him as he continued. "Oh my God, Dev," she repeated as white heat moved through her like a sweet burn. She climaxed again, this time clenching his cock, which felt so completely right, and emptying her mind.

She was dimly aware he'd gone still above her. His throat vibrated, part groan, part purr, which she adored, and he filled her. His head fell forward at a curiously vulnerable angle to his neck. As he began to sink down on her, she kissed that throat, licking at the skin covering the cartilage of his voice box, extraordinarily pleased at how satisfied he'd sounded when he groaned during his climax.

He rested there, on top of her, using his elbows to bear some of his weight, but seemingly unable to move. She idly stroked his back, exploring the muscles, the spine, the shoulder blades.

She wanted to say "don't leave me" again, but twice had been more than enough for her pride. So she settled for caressing him and laying kisses along his collarbone.

Chapter Twelve

He had to end this right. Dev rolled, taking Callie with him, and she ended up atop him. She'd said he made her warm and she felt warm right now. He lightly touched her hot cheeks, her swollen lips, and her eyes closed at his touch, so he tucked her head into his shoulder and ran fingers through her silky hair.

That she looked and acted utterly sated pleased him. A long time ago—he'd kind of forgotten since the idea of being asexual had invaded him—he'd liked women. A lot. Women had liked him. The memories had been shuttered closed and they were still vague, interfered with by many of Scott's instructions no doubt.

He stroked her hip and buttock. She was surprisingly muscular, in a sleek, sexy way. Ruth had said Callie liked big cats and he thought of how Callie moved with a strange, silent grace.

He would miss her. Given they'd only known each other three days, the harsh regret was a little absurd, but it sat there, inside him, very real, very painful. She had opened up his past for him. He wasn't asexual. *Scott* was, and wanted Dev to be.

His mind shied away from the no-doubt-complicated reasons for that. Later, he could explore them. Dev had other things to discover about himself.

She slid off, but remained in contact, curling around him,

now tracing patterns across his chest. She'd been unsure at first, after he'd kissed her, had seemed not quite certain about where to place hands or what to do. Probably related to her idea that sex was uncomfortable. He had to wonder about which assholes she'd gone to bed with. They hadn't deserved her and maybe he didn't either, but he could treasure her.

He kissed the top of her head and finally forced his thoughts to where they had to go. Hard work when he was never entirely sure which thoughts were his. But still necessary. Even now. Especially now.

"Callie?"

"Mmmm," she murmured, sounding as exhausted as he felt.

"I need you to do me a great favor."

Her finger that had been circling his nipple stopped moving.

"I'm sorry I have to ask you now, but, well, we don't have much time."

"Okay," she said in an encouraging if cautious way.

He nuzzled her temple, to soften the request. "I want you to take Madison and Ruth away from here first thing tomorrow morning."

She stiffened against him.

"Would you do that for me, Callie?"

She shook her head against his shoulder.

His heart sank. He'd hoped she would see how important it was that they go to safety. If his brain were working better, he could find the words to convince her this was the right action. He would simply have to work with what he had. He swallowed before speaking. "It's not safe here. I need to know you're all safe. It's very important to me. If you care about me at all, you'll do this. I think you care a little."

"I care," she said softly.

He pulled in a breath. "There's someone named Ian. He once lived here and I know where he lives now. I believe he would take you in. Help you all. He would recognize Madison, and you could tell him your story." He paused, not sure how to beg, though he would beg for this. "It would mean the world to me, Callie."

"I will take Madison and Ruth to Ian." She rested her palm on his sternum, right where the rib cage ended and the soft tissue began. "Then I'll come back. I won't leave you. In fact, it would be better if you came with us."

"We can't leave Scott like this," he said flatly, and he had to regret that the afterglow of sex had completely vanished. As pillow talk, this was terrible.

"I agree. But I'm the one he can't control, remember?"

He was too tired to rise up, but he rolled to the side so they could gaze at each other, even if it was hard to see her clearly in the darkness. "Why is that, do you think? As you well know, I assumed you were one of them, a Minder," he clarified, though he hated uttering the word, "when I saw that Scott didn't have you under his sway."

"I'm a puma, Dev." There was no teasing in her delivery. She seemed to regard this as a fact about herself and the cougar-as-sexually-aggressive-older-woman was obviously not what she was referring to. If he hadn't been so fog-brained from living as one of Scott's, he would have realized that from the beginning.

"What does being a puma mean?" he asked.

She hesitated and he could feel his eyelids droop shut. After this hellish day after a hellish year, followed by this startling sexual connection and the sex itself—well, he wasn't going to stay awake much longer.

"It's complicated but I'll show you some time, okay?"

He might have mumbled something. She kissed his mouth, then turned so he spooned her, and he sank into sleep.

For Dev, last night was supposed to have been about goodbye. He'd meant to explain to Callie just how important it was that she, Ruth and Madison get away. However, when she'd stepped into his room, his dick had become as hard as a rock and things had gotten away from him. He'd felt desperate to connect, and despite her uncertainty, she'd responded to his touch. Everything about their bodies coming together had felt right, when nothing had felt right for a long, long time.

She'd slept the night tucked against him, probably just as exhausted as he was, and though he was hard again, he edged backwards, away from her, and got out of bed. Silently he pulled on his shorts and eased open the door. Walked across to Ruth's room and stood outside the door. The door that led to Scott. Dev couldn't leave Scott like this, no matter how badly this past year had gone.

It wasn't quite compulsion. Dev had it within him to fight going to the boy. Yesterday he had quite successfully chosen not to speak to Scott, or perhaps more accurately not let Scott speak to him, *push* him. But it couldn't go on. It wasn't the first time he'd tried to rescue Scott and it might not be the last. There was something called responsibility. He placed his hand on the doorknob and turned it as quietly as possible, because if Callie heard him going to Scott, she'd intervene. Dev slipped inside the room and walked over, staring down at Scott whose fair skin was bruised by Callie's punch.

"Good morning, Scott," Dev said in a low voice.

Scott jerked awake with a gasp, blinking rapidly as he gained his bearings, then tried to clear the sleep from his eyes by squeezing them. He gave up and rubbed his free hand over his eyes, before turning his gaze back on Dev. Relief showed plainly as Scott gathered himself to talk.

"Don't speak yet, Scott."

As Scott went to open his mouth, Dev held up a hand, palm forward. "Really. If you ever owed me anything, don't speak now. It's better for me if you're quiet and I'm not trying to figure out whether or not I'm being pushed." Dev waited and after a moment, Scott nodded.

Dev let out a breath he hadn't realized he'd been holding. He might be a fool to think he could trust Scott and he might be fool to try to rescue him, and yet, he had to try. Yes, Scott had pulled him into this mess, but the kicker was, he wasn't the only one unwillingly caught in this hell. Scott, too, had been paying some kind of price with that fucking pod he belonged to. For longer than Dev had.

"I'm going to ask some yes-or-no questions. Nod or shake your head, okay?"

Scott nodded.

"Were you expected back yesterday? I know Eleanor keeps tabs on you."

Again Scott nodded.

"So she'll do something about your no-show, right?"

With a shaky sigh, Scott indicated yes.

Dev racked his stupid brain, trying to remember how the pod worked. It had been so long since he'd thought about the other Minders, mostly because thoughts about them made him even crazier than usual. He shivered a bit, remembering Max the enforcer who had liked to think of himself as their real leader, even if that role fell to Eleanor. Bile rose in Dev's throat and he tried to keep a leash on the rage that threatened to swamp him.

He turned his focus back on Scott. "Is Max likely on his way today?" Max did Eleanor's heavy work, Dev remembered that much.

Scott shrugged one shoulder, opening a palm to indicate it was possible. The pod was very big on obedience and rule following, and Scott not returning would be marked as an anomaly. Dev frowned, a bit disoriented by all this information suddenly available in his brain. Between Scott being restrained like this and Callie coming to his room and asking questions with her body and her voice, Dev was coming alive. It was going to be painful.

He was losing track of the crucial point of this conversation. *Focus, Dev.* Madison, Ruth and Callie *had* to get out of here before a member of Scott's pod arrived.

"Can you call the other Minders and say that everything here is A-okay at your house? Tell them you just want to hang out with your zombies."

Scott slowly shook his head. There was fear in his gaze and before Dev could stop him, Scott was saying, "Take these handcuffs *off.*"

Dev rocked back while Scott added, "I'm so sorry, Dev, but it's too late for phone calls. If Max gets here, he is going to kill me, kill us all. You need to get us all away from here. Callie understands *nothing.* I thought she was one of us, but she's not."

Shaking his head, Dev tried to concentrate. He had to think for a moment about what he was doing. Why hadn't he thought to release Scott? It was pathetic, the boy shackled to the bed.

Inhumane. How could he have been left here for an entire day? Dev hated seeing someone restrained like this.

"I'm sorry, I'm sorry," said Scott, wiping his face. The boy was crying and Dev tried to remember why. Why was Scott apologizing when he was handcuffed? "I have to get out of here. We all have to leave as soon as possible."

Out of nowhere, Callie slammed into the room, startling Dev afresh. He realized, with a terrible sinking sensation, that he was shaking. Goddammit.

Placing herself between Scott and Dev, she spoke to Scott, almost snarling. "You say another fucking word and I will punch your teeth out so you can't speak." Scott cowered back, raising an arm to protect his head. "I mean it, Scott."

She spun around to face Dev who blinked, uneasy with her threat, uneasy with his own spaciness. Something felt wrong, something always felt wrong.

"Why would you come to this room, Dev?" She found it painful, it seemed, to see him here and Dev tried to remember why. He was getting a headache.

Still he searched for an answer to Callie's question, because it was important to her, while she waited, patient, concerned. He found what he was looking for. This boy was his responsibility. "I'm worried about Scott. I owe him."

Callie stepped right up to Dev and before he could recall that he wasn't a passionate person, she kissed him full on the mouth. Last night came rushing back so vivid and with such a strong wave of relief that he curled a hand around the back of her head and kissed her, took control, mated his tongue with hers. Some of the noise in his head retreated and he didn't stop kissing while he skimmed a hand down to massage her breast.

She responded, arms wrapping around his shoulders, body leaning into his and he wanted to undress her, fuck her, make love to her.

The banging stopped him, shook him back to the present situation—Scott was tied up and needed to be freed. And yet... Dev pulled away from Callie to see Scott was jerking against his handcuffs, glaring at them both, but not speaking.

Then Dev remembered what was important and faced Callie again.

She had to get out of here. They all did.

"Max is likely on his way. He's going to kill Scott. We can't leave him like this."

She gazed at him, her amber eyes wide and full and shiny, like she was most worried about him, not Scott, and she said, "Will you let me talk to Scott by myself, Dev? If it's only me, I'll have no reason to hit him to shut him up."

Dev ran a hand through his hair, thinking, or trying to think. If nothing else, he needed to rouse Madison and Ruth, wake them up and prepare them for their departure. There was a lot to be done. So he nodded and left the room. After Callie shut the door behind him and Dev was out in the hall, he sank down to a crouch and bowed his head, feeling nauseated.

It had been a year now. A year of this sickening sensation. It happened when Scott pushed him. Scott was not supposed to push him. The original pact had been no pushing. What had happened to change that?

God. He couldn't even begin to sort it out. But he could act. Dev pulled himself up to standing and walked into Madison's room. He had to ensure the child reached safety.

Callie stalked up to Scott, loomed over him. "You have quite the influence over Dev, and you don't hesitate to use it. Congratulations."

"Dev cares about me." Scott lifted his chin, defiant.

"Right. You've told him to."

"He cared before I told him. He *cares*. The only one in the world probably."

You got that right. Callie chose not to speak the words.

Scott jerked his head towards the bathroom. "I have to piss. Bad."

"Tough. Piss yourself for all I care."

Scott's eyes blazed at her.

"You told me yesterday you wouldn't push Dev again."

He lunged towards her, not getting far. "You don't fucking understand. Max is coming here. He's going to take over—"

"And we're all going to die. Yes, I remember." She reached for the key in her pocket. Held it up. "I thought I was going to kill Max, wasn't that the plan?"

"If you won't let us leave." It was the raw panic in Scott's voice that got to her. She had no doubt he was frightened of Max. She undid the handcuff from the bed and waited for Scott to attack her. Instead, he rushed to the bathroom, which convinced her that his bladder had indeed been full. He re-emerged at the threshold of the bathroom and held up his arm with the handcuff dangling. "Would you take this off me?"

She shook her head.

"*Please,*" he whispered and something about his stance alerted her.

"Come here, Scott."

He bolted for the window and if she hadn't been Puma he might have made it, but she was fast, grabbing him before he hit the screen. How he planned to jump from the second story unhurt, she didn't ask. Instead, she dragged him backwards, threw him down on the bed and landed on him, squashing him as he flailed.

He wasn't particularly weak, but he had no strategy to fight her and she was strong. She pulled him up, clamping the handcuff to the bedframe's post. Then she jumped back, out of his reach and he stopped struggling, all the energy suddenly drained out of him. He just lay there, staring at the ceiling.

"Callie." His eyes were bright with unshed tears, and her protective instincts came roaring to the forefront. *Of all the crappy timing.* She didn't want to protect this one, who abused others. But he was terrified. "I'll do anything for you. *Anything.* Just let me go."

She didn't want to even guess what he was offering her, but the pleading made her uneasy. What she really wanted, needed, was answers.

"Tell me why Dev cares about you," she said flatly.

Chest heaving, Scott repositioned himself to sitting, pulling up his legs as if making himself smaller would protect him. He blinked gray eyes at her. "Dev was my big brother."

Callie frowned. "*Was?* Do siblings stop being siblings? I don't think so. Besides, you two don't look at all alike." Though neither did she and Ruth.

"Big. Brother. The organization. Looks out for boys without fathers and matches them up with a volunteer." Scott swallowed. "Dev became my Big Brother when I turned twelve." Callie thought there was some kind of pride in this statement. "He was for three years."

"Till you were fifteen. Then what happened?"

"Callie, we don't have time for me to recount our history."

"We do. I'm going to take care of Max." If she could take down feral cougars twice her size, admittedly with a bit of help—okay it was past time to call Trey for a consult—she could take care of this fucking Max. "What happened when you were fifteen?"

His gaze slid away from her. "They took me away."

"They?"

"The government. They decided something was wrong with me because I was messing with my teachers too much and it was getting obvious." He sneered and she realized he was sneering at himself. "I was stupid. Should have been a lot more careful. I was fifteen and I thought I was too clever by half and no one could touch me. I was a fucking *idiot*."

"Did you mess with Dev back then?"

"Not much. He was too nice and I had plenty of other people to work on. Once, I got Dev to buy me cigarettes and he was so upset afterwards I didn't want to do it again. Stuck to pushing for double helpings of dessert, which disconcerted him slightly, but he could shrug it off since I was skinny."

She didn't know if she totally believed Scott, but she was fascinated. "How did you meet up with Dev again? If they took you away."

Scott hung his head. "I phoned him, asked if I could crash at his place. Three years since he'd last seen me, and he didn't even hesitate. He said, 'of course'." Scott let out a long, painful sigh. "I just wanted to feel a little safe for a while. Then Max arrived on Dev's doorstep. *And he's going to arrive here again.*"

"I have a lot more questions, Scott, but first I'm going to get you some breakfast." *And get the others away. And phone Trey.* She didn't mind confronting Max, not at all. But she didn't want the others exposed to him.

Scott kept talking. "The reason Dev doesn't leave me is because he feels responsible for me, because he was my Big Brother. I think he genuinely liked me at one time."

She could not respond to the hopeful wistfulness in his voice. Could not. Later maybe, if she was able to sort him out when he wasn't a threat to others.

"If that's true, why have you messed with Dev so much? You're ruining him, Scott. You must know that."

"I had no choice. Max left me with no choice."

"Well. I'll take it up with Max then."

"He's strong."

Callie smiled. "Ruth says I'm strong."

Chapter Thirteen

"I can't leave the house," Ruth repeated. Her incredulous tone suggested that Callie was asking her to do the impossible, like go to the moon. Her echo of Dev's own "can't leave" suggested that Scott had been at work here.

Hands on hips, Callie turned to Dev. "Someone explain to me why Ruth *can't leave.*"

Dev just looked away. Since he wanted Callie to leave too, he didn't seem inclined to help with explanations right now. Madison stood there, beside Dev's car, and she piped up. "Scott told Ruth not to leave." Madison delivered this information as if this explained everything, and Callie supposed it did.

"Okay." Callie jiggled the car keys that Ruth refused to take. Madison and Ruth's bags were packed and in the car. Only at the moment of departure had Ruth suddenly realized she could not get in the car. "Ruth, why doesn't Scott want you to go?"

"He's taking care of me." Ruth bit her lip. "I was actually quite sick, Callie."

"I understand that." Callie decided it wasn't the time to point out that Scott could no longer take care of Ruth, given that Scott was imprisoned in her old bedroom. "You're healthy now." Callie walked over and gave Ruth a big hug. "Could you leave for me?"

Ruth shook her head, tears starting in her eyes, and Callie was a little afraid her sister would turn hysterical which wasn't optimal when she needed to make a two-hour drive.

"You're no longer sick, Ruth," Dev said quietly. "That's what Scott wanted, to make you better. Ian, the man you're going to visit, was also sick, and when he became healthy, he too left. Do you believe Scott wanted to give you a safe place to recuperate from your sickness?"

"Yes," declared Ruth, and her sister's fervor disturbed Callie.

"And he has." Dev gestured to his car. "Now you have to go because..." he gave a long sigh, "...Max is coming and Scott doesn't want you to see Max again."

"Who's Max?" Ruth reacted to the name, going pale.

"You don't want to know," Dev said. "Do you believe me, that Scott doesn't want you to see Max?"

"Yes. If I could just talk to Scott, to make sure." Ruth had put in this request three times already, but again she reached for Callie. Despite her sister's pleading, Callie couldn't risk Scott pushing Ruth. The Minder was too unpredictable.

"Trust me, Ruth. Please." Callie tucked a stray lock of hair behind Ruth's ear. "Scott wants us all out of the house before Max comes." Here she improvised, playing with the truth, because Callie really wanted to take down Max. Without these normals around. "We need to scatter a bit, it's safer that way. We'll be harder to find." She opened Ruth's clenched fist, placing the car keys in her palm, and she accepted them.

"Okay." Ruth tossed the keys in the air once, caught them. "Right. Let's do it." She held out a hand for Madison. "Come on, kid. If I can't trust my sister, I can't trust anyone."

There was another flurry of hugs, as Madison clung to Dev and Ruth threw herself at Callie. Then Ruth slid into the driver's seat while Dev set Madison in the booster seat and buckled her in. He slammed the door, Ruth started the engine and they backed down the drive before taking off down the street. Once they were out of sight, Callie turned to Dev. "What the hell am I going to do with you?"

His gaze turned dark. "Nothing," he warned.

"You need to get away from here. You should have gone with them." They were both furious with the other for not leaving. Callie could not understand why Dev didn't see he was much more susceptible than she was. What was going through his brain? If Max was as lethal as Scott claimed, Dev must have some kind of death wish. He also didn't seem to believe that Callie could hold her own against Max.

Not that Dev said any of that. Instead, he observed, "Ruth actually wants to go. She has no real bond with Scott outside of what he's pushed on her."

Bond? Real? Did that mean Dev believed *he* had one with Scott? Jesus. "That's fucking great, but I don't want you going anywhere near Scott so he can push *you*, Dev."

He pulled her to him, wrapped his arms around her, breathed in her hair. "I don't know why, but when I touch you, when you touch me, I can remember things about myself, I can remember who I am." He molded her body against his.

"I'm scared about what other ideas Scott has planted in your head. Because you sure as hell aren't *asexual.*"

"I've figured that much out." His wry words were incredibly endearing. He brushed lips across her forehead, feathering kisses over her eyes and face, before reaching her neck. She shivered in his arms, then pushed herself away.

He let her put some space between them, but still held her in the safe cage of his arms as he looked at her. "I want you to leave. Max is dangerous."

"*Fuck*," she swore, sick of this circling conversation where they both apparently wanted to fall on the sword for the other. Except that she had the tools to turn that metaphorical sword on Max, if it came down to it. "What about you? Isn't he more dangerous to you?"

"Give me the key to the handcuffs. Scott and I will also flee. But you will be safer without us." Dev's gaze sharpened. "The Minders don't know about you yet, Callie, and I want to keep it that way."

She tilted her head. "Why can't you leave? What kind of hold does Scott have on you? Ruth left but you can't. Is it because you've known Scott longer?"

Dev looked sad. "I won't leave. Everyone else has abandoned him and a long time ago I promised him I wouldn't."

"He *made* you promise him, Dev. He forced that promise out of you. It's not really yours. Don't you realize that?" She was pleading now. She wished she knew how to get through to him.

A brief shake of the head. Dev refused to be turned away from his belief. "I think you're wrong."

She closed her eyes. How could she argue with this, this *compulsion*. It seemed impossible.

"I was once his Big Brother, Callie."

"I know that," she snapped. "He told me. You don't think he pushed you then?"

"I don't think he pushed me then, no. Because I had a normal life then."

She decided not to mention the cigarette-buying incident. Dev would dismiss it as an anomaly or unimportant. "Okay, okay. Say that's true, that he didn't push you when he was younger. Obviously that phase is over. Scott is no longer a boy, and he's messed with you too much. Can't you see it? Feel it?"

She gripped him harder and tried another tack. "*I* will look after Scott. I'll do my best. That is my promise and my promises mean something, Dev. They aren't empty." Besides, she wanted to save Scott, if she could. Scott was a fellow freak, and if Callie hadn't been able to help that young male cougar last year, perhaps she could save Scott who at least didn't seem to kill people. Yet.

"I once told a young teenager that he could always count on me, could always come to me for help." Dev winced at the memory. "He was abused, Callie."

"He's abused *you*, Dev."

Dev didn't react, just set his jaw, but she waited him out, until he finally admitted, "Perhaps."

"Perhaps? Come on."

He shrugged, stepping away, and she wished they didn't have to argue this. "I can't leave him like that, Callie. Maybe it's because he's compelled me, maybe it's because I was once responsible for him. Maybe both. But I. Cannot. Leave. I won't."

She pulled in a breath and wished she could physically force him away from here. "Let's go back inside. Figure this out."

They marched up the front steps, both weary of the same argument. Callie had the impression that Dev was trying to communicate with her as much as she with him. If only Scott's "pushes" weren't in the mix and she could see Dev's point of view as his own. However, Dev's point of view was also Scott's.

They entered the front hallway, and Callie decided to share some of her conversation with Scott. See what Dev made of it. She turned, placing a hand on Dev's arm. "Scott wants me to kill Max. I don't know if I will, but I'm going to give it serious consideration."

Dev had gone a little pale, rather like Ruth earlier. Their

reaction made Callie feel quite grim. She'd have to be careful about who she was facing, because Max seemed dangerous. He certainly knew how to evoke fear in people.

"Who is Max, Dev?"

"He's bad." Dev closed his eyes. "I don't remember him clearly. I'm probably not supposed to. I can't remember his features at all. Might be a little taller than me. Maybe."

"I'm strong."

"That's what Ruth said, but I don't know what she means. Besides, being able to beat up Max is not how you win against someone like him."

"I'm a puma."

He frowned. "I *really* don't know what you mean by that."

"Have you heard of werewolves?"

"Sure," he said slowly.

"Like that. Only I shift into a cougar, a puma." The puma in her didn't like her giving the cougar example first. Her cat had always been quite adamant about her real name. But they called the big cats cougars up here.

It was quite evident by Dev's expression that he didn't believe her, didn't know why she had told him this bizarre lie. Callie figured they just didn't have time to work this out now. A real-life demonstration in the future perhaps, when life was a little less stressful, when the threat of Max had been neutralized.

Dev clenched a fist suddenly and locked gazes with her. "I can't stand Scott being up there like that anymore. It really bothers me."

"He pushed you this morning, Dev."

His eyes widened as if just remembering. He gazed at her warily. "Are you sure?"

"I'm sure. It's why you're so upset about him being handcuffed in that room. Thing is, I don't think you should be pushed again. *Ever.*"

Dev's gaze darkened, with lust, she realized, though why that declaration should turn him on, she didn't know. He closed the distance between them.

"I'm thinking," he said in a low voice, "that a quickie might clear my head." He slid an arm around her waist and smoothed hair away from her face. "I don't know what the fuck to make of your talk about pumas, and I don't know what the fuck to do about Scott who I *know* I can't trust, but who I still want to help." He nuzzled her neck, before tracing her collarbone with his tongue. "What I do know is that I want you."

"Dev," she murmured, melting into him.

If she hadn't been so focused on Dev and his mouth and his hands, she would have noticed the intruder before he entered the house. He'd snuck in the back door and crossed through the kitchen before she even broke away from Dev to find a stranger standing in the hall facing them both. A slight smile played on his face. Recognizing a predator instantly, Puma went on high alert.

"Don't move an inch, Dev," the man commanded, and Dev froze, only his chest moving as he breathed too hard. Callie thought, *Oh God, it's Max.* He pointed at Callie. "You don't move either, unless I tell you to."

Callie stiffened, which Max took to be a good thing, because his smile broadened and that smile turned ugly, feral. "Aren't you a pretty thing? Where'd you come from?"

She blinked at the asshole.

"I asked you a fucking question. You answer. Where are you from?"

"The forest," Callie said unthinkingly.

The brown-haired, brown-eyed man gestured impatiently, annoyed by her response. "Give me your name."

"Callie."

"Callie who?"

"Just Callie." She'd actually taken Ruth's last name, way back when, but Callie was the only name she felt belonged to her.

Frowning, Max directed his question at Dev. "Who is she?"

Uninflected answer, though Dev was trembling. "Ruth's sister."

"Heh. I like to do sisters. Where's Ruth, Callie?"

She opened her mouth to explain that Ruth was on her way to Ian's with Madison, then clamped her mouth shut. *God.* Max was working on her and she could feel it, the strain in her body. The puma in her was snarling at Max's sudden leash on her, was enraged by the control and how Callie hadn't noticed. That anger broke like a wave over Callie and the spell cracked open. Callie came back to herself. "None of your fucking business. *Max.*"

He drew himself up and her puma brain screeched, *Danger.*

They were in the hall and the only thing Callie could pick up as a weapon was a stool by the phone. She stepped towards Max, lifting the stool as she moved, and swung it down on him. He barely had time to lift his arm, trying to protect his head.

He crumpled against the wall.

"Dev," Callie shouted. "Get out of here." She glanced at him. He was glassy-eyed from the push and didn't budge an inch.

She turned back to Max and time slowed to a painful crawl. Blood ran down the side of his face—he was wincing from the pain—but a gun was now gripped in his hand and it exploded.

Pain stabbed into her chest and her body jerked back. Her shoulders hit the wall and her knees began to give out.

Fucking idiot, she thought as she slid down the wall and hit the floor. She plastered a hand across her chest. A lung was pierced, but her heart, thank God, was still beating. She could shift.

She'd wanted to get Dev away from the monster. Instead she'd condemned her lover to a terrible fate, to Max's whim. She started to fade as Puma screamed and clawed its way to the surface, determined to survive this assault. The last Callie could remember was crawling into the kitchen as Max's voice assaulted Dev.

"You have nothing to fucking cry about, Dev."

Dev wasn't sure where the voice came from. He tried to focus. Couldn't remember why he had tears running down his face. How embarrassing.

A palm slammed across his cheek, making his head swerve to the side. It came again from the other side and Max laughed.

Oh yes, Dev remembered Max. Though he couldn't remember why Max's cheek was split open and bleeding.

"You deserved that, for letting that bitch into this house. Don't you agree, Dev?"

Max was usually right so Dev nodded.

"Look at me, you moron."

Dev forced his gaze on Max, who was bruised and bleeding. Where had the blood come from? Max never let anyone hurt him.

"Someone tried to kill me, Dev."

Dev tried to process those words, but who could possibly kill Max? The Minder was now wiping down a gun. Dev frowned at that and Max managed an awful grin.

"Don't want my fingerprints on it, see? Just yours. *You* want your fingerprints on the gun. Because you are going to kill that girl, shoot her in the head."

Dev's vision began to turn black and Max gripped him by the shoulder, shaking him.

"You do not faint on me, Dev. You stay conscious and do exactly as I say. You are going to take this gun, follow that trail of blood"—Max grabbed the back of Dev's neck and jerked Dev's gaze towards an awful line of bright red that led to the kitchen—"and you are going to shoot that bitch Callie in the head. Because you don't like violence and she tried to kill me. She's dangerous, Dev."

Dev couldn't remember where he was so he closed his eyes.

"*Wake up, Dev.*"

He blinked awake.

"Tell me where Scott is."

Dev frowned. He didn't want Max to see Scott. Scott was terrified of Max and Scott's terror hurt Dev.

Max grabbed Dev's face, forcing him to look straight into his eyes. "God, you're resistant. What the fuck is wrong with you? Where is Scott? You tell me."

Dev's mouth seemed to work on its own. Someone else spoke the words for him, because he didn't want to. "Scott is upstairs in one of the bedrooms."

"Good enough." Max put a gun, of all things, in Dev's hand. Where had the gun come from? "It's all set," said Max, as if Dev knew what he was talking about. "You just pull the trigger." Once again, Max forced their gazes to lock and Dev tried not to recoil though he hated looking into those eyes. "You, Dev, are going to press the muzzle of this gun against Callie-from-the-forest's forehead and you are going to pull the trigger. Kill her."

Dev thought he might throw up. Max just patted his cheek and then bounded up the stairs. Halfway up, he stopped and looked down at Dev who hadn't moved. "Tell me what you're going to do," Max said softly.

Something jerked his mouth open and formed words: "Go to the kitchen. Pull the trigger."

"Excellent." Max continued up and Dev looked down at the trail of blood.

He followed it into the kitchen. From far, far away, a voice screamed his name in terror, and Dev remembered Scott was somewhere, but first he had a task to accomplish. If he could remember what it was. His memory was shit. So easily distracted. Despite Max's instructions, Dev found himself listening for Scott, but only heard silence. Then he forgot everything, lost in time and space.

He didn't know how long he stood there, unaware of what was going on, but the sound of purring entered his consciousness and he focused on the here and now. Gazing down, he saw a large cougar spread out on its side on the kitchen floor. It seemed shaken and...bloody. The poor thing had been shot, although Dev was finding it difficult to reconcile the newly healed bullet wound with the fresh blood on the floor. He shifted his gaze to stare into amber eyes and found them oddly familiar.

The purring continued and the cat rose, rather gingerly, to rub itself against his thigh. He went to pat it and realized he had a fucking gun in his hand.

"Jesus!" How could he forget a gun? His whole body began to shake as he tried to figure out what the fuck was going on. The cat continued to push against him in, he thought, affection, and with his free hand he did pat it. She—the cat seemed like a she, something about the eyes—took delight in the contact. Then collapsed on the floor. Perhaps the wound was worse than he thought.

He wished he could let go of the gun. He was so tired.

The cat seemed to go straight to sleep, and Dev's vision began to blur or something, because the cat kept going in and out of focus, its body no longer quite cougar shaped. Even the fur was disappearing.

Dev was going insane, hallucinating.

From upstairs, someone screamed, startling Dev, and something within him came alive. Memories, jumbled and nonsensical, flashed before him. There were many things he was supposed to do, but the one that pushed at him most strongly was to protect Scott. Grimly he turned away from the blurry, imaginary cat and marched up the stairs.

The trigger, pull the trigger. An image of Callie flashed before his eyes and he stiffened before he dragged himself forward. The compulsion to turn and harm Callie hurt him, caused him pain, and he fought against it. He could resist. After all, he had been with Minders too long. Understood that their compulsions didn't always work, especially when he fought. And fight he would. Most significantly, he recognized that the desire to shoot a lover could never belong to him. He did not inflict damage on those he made love to.

Besides, he thought, his mind taking an easier route than straight rejection of the push, Callie was gone. Escaped. Left her beloved cat in her wake. She loved cats though Dev couldn't remember why.

The door to Ruth's room, the door leading to Scott, had been left ajar, and Dev pushed it open.

Scott was weeping on the bed, nose bleeding, blood smeared on his hand. Max enjoyed beating people up and Dev didn't like that. Somewhere within, the anger built, forcing out everything else that had been pushed on him.

Because Scott was naked too, and that made Dev furious. Scott didn't like to be naked. Nudity scared Scott. He didn't like touch much either. There were reasons for these fears, an ugly history that Dev could no longer remember.

Max was grinning down at Scott and Dev didn't quite understand, because Max liked women. Then again, he also liked to torment and humiliate.

"Touch yourself, Scott. Touch your limp dick." Max, who liked to enforce anything he damn pleased, was pushing Scott. The boy shook his head, his expression cringing, even while his hand crept down towards his crotch. He froze, catching sight of Dev in the doorway. Mistake, because Max realized they weren't alone and spun to face Dev.

No time. Act. Dev pulled the trigger. Hit Max's shoulder. Max moved his mouth to speak but Dev could not allow the enforcer's words to push at him, not again. So this time Dev aimed properly, with two hands, aimed straight at that evil mouth. Pulled the trigger again. Hit the target before the words were formed.

Max's head jerked back and he dropped to the floor, crumpling at the foot of the bed. Noise roared in Dev's head, but not the noise of gunshots. Those had been silent. Dev stared at the body, at the blood blooming, already spreading across the hardwood floor. He tried to make sense of the scene, even if he had created it, even if he still had that gun pointed at Max. How could Max have been shot? Dev couldn't quite remember. He was supposed to have put the muzzle of the gun against a forehead, but Dev had aimed for the mouth. *Max's* mouth, that could wreak no further damage. Dev didn't really want to look at the enforcer anymore. Didn't really want to look anywhere.

He heard sniveling in the background and was aware of Scott yanking clothes back on. Good, that meant someone had removed Scott's handcuffs. Dev had wanted those damned handcuffs off the boy.

"My fingerprints are on the gun," Dev said to no one in particular.

Chapter Fourteen

Callie dragged herself up the stairs. Despite the fact that she heard only two voices, Scott's and Dev's, she was terrified about what she might find. The puma in her was fighting to take control again, but Callie refused to yield. Two shifts in such a short period of time was exhausting and her body could not face a third right now. Besides, the human was desperate to find Dev.

From the doorway she saw a tearstained Scott who had never looked younger and a shell-shocked Dev who appeared to be staring out the window. On the floor lay a very bloody Max, his face shot out. Red stained the wood beneath him. It was an awful, mesmerizing sight. Even Puma was stunned.

"Dev?" she said softly.

He spun and dropped the gun he was holding, the same gun that had shot a now-healing hole in her chest. It was still tender. "Christ, Callie, don't come near me or I might shoot you in the forehead."

She blinked at that odd comment. "Dev, you just dropped the gun." She pointed to the floor. "You're not going to shoot me."

Dev looked at his empty hand, baffled.

Huddled beside Dev, Scott gazed at Callie from across the room. She supposed she had better tell him not to speak again, given that Dev was in the room and not doing great after the Max encounter.

Scott opened his mouth and she raised her hand.

"I have no intention of pushing anyone," Scott said wearily. "I wanted to explain that Max probably told Dev to shoot you. In the forehead."

Dev's expression became even more troubled.

"Well, he's not doing a very good job of it," Callie observed.

The joke fell flat. Dev stared at her, a little wild-eyed now, and she went to him. He took her in a bruising hug, even while he was shaking so.

"Hey," she said soothingly, "you couldn't even punch me when Scott told you to. What makes you think you could shoot me?"

"Max is stronger than I am and he likes to break people," Scott supplied helpfully. But his voice cracked and he wiped his face.

Callie pulled back. This was no time to get lost in Dev's touch. Already today she had been distracted by him when she should have protected everyone.

"Max won't be breaking anyone anymore," she pointed out.

Scott shook off her reassurance. "There will be Eleanor to deal with once she realizes Max hasn't returned home. She'll bring backup."

"More Minders?" When Scott just nodded she looked at Dev. He didn't speak, simply moved behind her and hugged her from the back.

Scott watched their interaction a little warily and she had the sense he didn't like her standing between him and Dev. Like it or not, it was time to make one thing crystal clear to this pale, trembling boy. Because she was ready to destroy the next person who forced Dev, no matter how vulnerable Scott seemed right now.

"Scott, if you want to be with us at all, you have to promise you will *never* push Dev again." She was close to snarling, she knew. "If you do, I am likely to kill you, though I don't want to. Do you understand me?"

Scott held up his hands, palms facing her. "I promise, I promise." Maybe he meant it. "Just don't leave me behind."

She frowned at his request. "Why not? Why don't you want to stay with your kind?"

"They're not my kind," Scott spat. "I hate them. I'm not like Max."

"Okay," she allowed. "Aren't you drawn to them?" For better or worse, she was drawn to her fellow werecougars. "Won't they welcome you? You could just make up a story about being ambushed by me and Dev."

"Won't work," Dev murmured into her ear while Scott laughed, a high, forced sound with no humor in it.

"I can't *make up* a story," the boy said. "They'll force the truth out of me. Eleanor is stronger than anyone I've ever met." His voice dropped. "She controls me when I'm around her. I'm *her* zombie though technically Minders can't be zombies."

"Scott comes with us," declared Dev. While Scott cast him a look of gratitude, Callie couldn't help but wonder why Dev insisted on Scott's company. It made her suspicious. "If nothing else, Callie, you don't want him telling Eleanor where Ruth and Madison are."

Okay, that was something she hadn't considered. She decided not to argue against Scott coming along. Besides, she was hard-pressed to leave Scott with someone worse than Max. Despite her earlier words about killing the boy—something she'd only consider as a last resort—she had begun to feel

172

responsible for the lost, dangerous youth.

"You can come with us," agreed Callie, "if you do not push. If you do, if I ever find a *shred* of evidence that you have done it—"

"Okay, no more talk of killing, Callie." Sounding exhausted, Dev rested his chin on her shoulder. "I think Scott's got the message."

It was true, that Scott seemed desperate and shaky. Which might have reassured her if she were not so furious about what had happened to Dev. And here he was once again, trying to defend Scott.

"Jesus, Dev, this kid has backtracked on you how many times?" She didn't take her eyes off Scott who seemed to cringe. He was either an excellent actor or extremely frightened. "And you're going to just blithely go along with him again?"

Dev nuzzled her neck, for her reassurance or his, she wasn't sure. "I'm not *blithely* going along with anything, given that you're going to *kill* him."

"*I won't push Dev.* I won't. I won't." Scott swiped his face, trying to stop his crying. With his effort to contain himself, the rest of his words came out uneven and breathless. "It's like I said before, we have to get out of here. Eleanor will send others to investigate, might even come herself if she's pissed off enough. Minders go haywire when one of their own is taken down. Very protective in their fucked-up way."

Callie craned her neck to look over at Max and couldn't help but think she'd be glad to get far away from this body and its smell of death. However, she should get a better idea of what they were running from.

"How many are there of you?"

"Four to seven, depending." As she frowned, Scott added, "Some travel. Eleanor will be watching out for Max, expecting to hear from him. Eleanor." He whispered the name with some dread and Callie was reminded of his dire warning yesterday when it came to Max. She'd thought Scott was histrionic, but histrionic or not, Max had been pretty awful. Best to assume Eleanor was too.

"Well, we are not going to hang around here waiting for Eleanor like we did for Max." Callie turned to Dev who was now zoning out. He just closed his eyes and hugged her again. Hugs were good, but she didn't like his blank face.

"What's the matter with Dev?" she demanded of Scott.

"He doesn't like Eleanor any better than I do. Even her spoken name probably messes him up."

"I thought Max was the big bogeyman."

Scott looked up at her with some distaste. "They're all bad. Max was just the most gleeful about it. Eleanor is actually more deadly. She'd have killed you and Dev by now, whereas Max liked to *play*."

"All righty. Cheerful group of people, this pod of yours."

Scott cleared his throat. "We don't have much time."

She turned in Dev's arms, facing Scott again. "I don't trust you. So, you pack your car, with your stuff and Dev's stuff."

He nodded, seemingly fine with being ordered about by her. "You don't have anything to bring?"

Inwardly she laughed, wondering how he'd take to knowing she'd arrived as a puma, carrying nothing. "No, but I'll grab some of Ruth's leftovers. You, Dev, come with me. I have to call a friend." She tugged on Dev's arm, and he obediently followed her out of the room and down the stairs. She didn't like how unthinking he was.

"Who is your friend?" asked Dev as she picked up the phone in the hall. He'd taken a couple of minutes to process her last sentence and respond, but at least he'd processed.

"Trey Walters. My only friend."

He blinked, becoming more alert. "Hey. *I* am your friend."

Callie smiled, made slightly giddy by that simple declaration, and kissed him. Then she dialed in the number she hadn't forgotten during her time as puma.

Trey didn't pick up until the fourth ring, at which point Callie sagged against the wall with relief, thinking, *thank God.* With a dead body upstairs and a mind-control boy packing up for them, and Dev, who needed a fucking break from the mind games before his brain went on permanent leave—well, Callie felt desperate for some guidance.

"What's wrong," Trey demanded, and if it wasn't the friendliest greeting in the world, the concern in his voice warmed her.

"I have a big problem."

"Go ahead."

She swallowed, not quite sure how to start.

"Callie," he said impatiently, "are you in danger?"

"Not at the moment." She braced herself before asking, "Have you ever heard of people called Minders?"

"*Fuck.*"

She took that as a yes, but he didn't elaborate. "Um, Trey?"

"Where are you?"

"In Barrieville. At my sister's. Well, actually it's not her house—"

"A Minder's?" Trey asked sharply.

"No, though one came to visit, but it's a long story and there's a dead Minder upstairs. Not the one who came to visit." God, could she not present this information more clearly?

"Did you kill the dead Minder?"

"No. My friend Dev did. After the dead guy told Dev to kill me."

"*Fuck.*" Even more intense than the first time he swore. "How'd you get mixed up with them?"

"Ruth."

"Ruth is one of their zombies." It wasn't a question.

Callie cringed at that description of Ruth. "Yes. Or, she was."

"Tell me everything. From the beginning. As quickly as possible."

So she told the whole story from start to finish and Trey didn't interrupt her once. In fact, she stopped to ask if he was still there and, his voice sounding on edge, he told her to go on.

"Okay," he said when she was done. "Dead body in the bedroom and a pod of Minders how close?"

Pod? God, Trey knew their lingo. "You know about these kind of people?" she asked, flabbergasted.

"Of course I do. I was hunting them when I first found you. Not very successfully I might add. Though Ruth had given me pause."

"Had given you pause? Ruth? What do you mean? Trey, that was four years ago."

"Some of these Minders are more subtle than others. With their abilities, they're good at hiding in plain sight. This Max was obviously a bludgeon, which would have helped my finding them. Perhaps he wasn't around when I was trying to sniff them out." Trey paused. "Your sister had some of the qualities of a zombie.

"Callie, they'll kill you, because they can't control you and you know about them. Get the hell out. There's a safe house four hours east of where you are. Go there now, and I will meet up with you as soon as I can get a flight out of here. Don't tell anyone else about it, don't talk to anyone."

"I have to bring Dev and Scott."

After a pointed silence, Trey demanded quietly, "Why hang out with a Minder and his zombie, Callie?"

Not the time to argue that Dev and Scott couldn't be left behind. Callie didn't answer, she just waited Trey out. She'd done that occasionally, though it pissed him off, her using his technique against him.

Trey swore to himself before asking, "Any chance you'll change your mind on this?"

"None. I have to protect them."

"Cats."

Callie frowned. She was the only cat he knew. Before she could question him on that, he was moving on, accepting that Dev and Scott were involved. "I won't waste time thrashing this out with you. You better know what you're doing, bringing them along." Trey gave her the address and directions, told her to get out of the house *now.* "I am warning you one more time. You cannot trust that Minder, even if he's young, even if, *especially* if, he's been abused by other Minders. Those guys mess with each other's heads and the result is not pretty. Watch your back. You can't, unfortunately, trust a zombie either. If they're bonded to their Minder, they're unpredictable. It's a real mindfuck, Callie, I'm warning you."

"I'll be careful," she promised, looking at Dev who simply gazed back at her, expression still a little vacant, even if his eyes were warm.

"Go." Trey hung up.

Dev had listened to her carefully the entire time. Really he seemed a bit more himself now, not so shocky. But Trey's warning that zombies were unpredictable worried her. Because, yeah, Dev was obviously *bonded*—God, what a word—to Scott. Even if she refused to think of Dev as a true zombie. What had Scott called him? A fighter.

"Trey agrees with Scott," she told Dev. "We have to get the hell out now. He knows a safe place we can go."

Dev eyed her. "You sure you can trust this Trey and his judgment?"

"More than anyone I know. It's Scott I'm worried about. You need a break from him."

Dev's mouth twisted into a humorless smile, but he didn't say anything.

"Trey's going to meet us. He'll know what to do."

"What's so special about this Trey?"

"He fixes people's problems." *Or kills them.* But she didn't add that.

Chapter Fifteen

The drive east took too long. Callie supposed that four hours wasn't an unreasonable length of time to sit in the passenger seat, but she'd never liked being cooped up in a car, and Scott's Toyota Echo was small.

"Okay?" asked Dev for the third time. He was driving, Callie was in the front seat and Scott was laid out in the back, faking sleep or perhaps attempting it given that his chest rose and fell too hard. An arm was slung across his face.

"Sure." Callie tried to smile despite feeling carsick and anxious. Dev glanced down at her hands and she unclenched her fists, again.

"Is it the, uh, general situation that's bothering, or do you not like cars?"

"Both."

"Been in an accident?"

"Nope." She lowered her voice. "My cat doesn't like it."

"You have a cat?" came Scott's voice from the back.

"Sometimes." Callie didn't intend to elaborate.

"Where is it now?" he persisted. "Did you just abandon it?"

"None of your business, and no."

"Oh yeah, I'm not supposed to talk."

"That's right," Callie agreed. "So, quiet now." She searched through some CDs and shoved one in. They listened to guitar and a strained voice singing about some girl, but it was better than having Scott talk.

Eventually, it felt like years later to Callie, they drove off the highway and made their way into a suburb, found a dead-end street with a park beside the safe house and pulled into the driveway. As soon as they stopped, Scott pushed himself up to sitting and jumped out of the car. As did Callie.

He stared at the rather nondescript two-storey. "Hey, how are we supposed to get into the house?"

"I have the secret password," Callie drawled. At Scott's frown, she added, "Watch and learn." She strode up to the garage-door number pad and punched in the code Trey had given her over the phone. The door lurched into movement, folding up into the ceiling of a very neat garage. Dev drove the Echo in and they followed him.

With that, they carried what little they'd brought from the car and filed into the house to explore its small, blandly furnished rooms.

"Where's your friend?" asked Scott, who'd been told they were going to stay with someone Callie knew.

"Enough questions," Callie snapped.

Scott's expression turned sullen.

"Look, Scott." Callie walked right up to him. He was about three inches taller than her but easy to intimidate. She could see him shrink back from her. "You don't want to strike out on your own, you want to be with us, so you do so on *my* terms."

Scott's chin jutted out. "Dev doesn't have a say? It's all *your* terms?"

"You are so not the one to question me on that," she said

softly, and Scott had the grace to flush. "Now grab something from the kitchen. Trey said it would be stocked with food. Then go upstairs and choose a room. Dev and I have some talking to do, and no, you won't be a part of that conversation, because I can't be on guard against you all the time. It wears me out."

Scott's expression switched from resentful to earnest. "I promised you I wouldn't push Dev." He spoke as if he was hurt by her suspicions, which just made her groan.

"Thing is, Scott"—Dev's voice was flat—"you've promised me that before. Quite frankly, I need a break from you." It was one of the few times this trip Dev had addressed Scott directly. He wouldn't abandon the boy, but there was a kind of distaste in his tone.

Scott stomped off into the kitchen.

Dev hefted his bag and Callie's. "I'll go choose us a room." His eyes darkened a little as he held her gaze a beat. "And a bed."

"Sounds good." She intended they go to bed early tonight, and not just to sleep. There was a need to connect to Dev burning inside her and she could see it reflected in his dark, tormented eyes.

They ate dinner, without Scott. Callie didn't care that he was lonely and wanted to be with Dev. It wasn't that she didn't feel sorry for him. Scott looked quite frankly traumatized. She just didn't have the energy to guard against his words when he was around. Not only was that tiring, it was simply too dangerous for Dev, and he didn't argue the point.

After eating, they each showered and went to bed, Callie

firmly closing the door to the room she and Dev were sharing while Scott went off to his newly claimed bedroom. It was early but they were all exhausted by the events of the day, and the long drive that had followed.

"He's lonely. Badly lonely, in fact." Dev lifted his chin towards the door, indicating Scott.

"I know, but..." She threw out her hands in a what-can-I-do gesture. "We can't trust him."

"Perhaps not," Dev murmured, and it worried her that he could doubt that. It also worried her that he'd told her Scott was lonely at least four times today. It made her wonder if Scott had planted the idea there. Minder plants, as she'd begun to think of them, tended to get repeated by their zombies.

Zombie. God, she hated that word. It was dehumanizing. Dev was everything human at the moment. In fact, as he prowled around the room in his restless way, he made her think *panther*, which was odd given that she was the big cat. When they were alone, in the bedroom, and his eyes went dark, something changed between them.

He halted a few feet away and fixed his gaze on her, and she stopped worrying about him. Instead she went hot and cold all over because of the way he looked at her, like he wanted her and nothing else in the world.

She stood perfectly still, waiting. The intent there, that sat in his eyes, amazed her. She'd been with men before, when the craving for intimacy was too great, but she'd never felt like she had been the focus, only that the act had been.

Dev stalked up to her to hold himself a mere inch away, not quite touching, though she could feel his heat and he could feel hers. Bringing his hands to rest on her shoulders, he caressed the bare skin, then skimmed palms down her arms. She couldn't help herself, she shivered.

"In such a short time, you have become very special to me, Callie." He seemed almost puzzled by his statement. "How did you do that?"

She leaned forward into him, resting her face against his shoulder, breathing in his scent. "I think I was made to find you."

"Made to find me?" There was question in his low voice, but no censure, no amusement. He brushed lips over her forehead and tipped her chin up so he could gaze at her.

She had a hard time putting in words what she meant. "It's just that I've failed at so many things. You can't know." That last failure, the young, dead werecougar, still burned, still hurt. She'd wanted to save him.

On the other hand, she didn't want to save Dev so much as love him. Though she would save him too. From these god-awful Minders.

The amazing thing was, Dev appeared to want to save her as well, in his misguided attempts to get her to leave him. She rubbed her face against him and he stroked her head.

When she pulled back to look at him, he was still frowning, a kind of protest in his expression.

"I doubt that's true, about you failing." He brushed hair off her face. "People who are very hard on themselves say that."

"Perhaps." She offered him a wry smile. "So do people who fail."

"Not always. I still don't understand how you were made to find me. Even if I'm glad you are here."

How to explain how lost she became when she was on her own as Puma? How it seemed a miracle that he'd been with Ruth and they'd connected? Well, she couldn't. So instead she said, "I am one of the few people who can separate Scott from you, and it needed to be done. Even if you feel responsible for him."

His face went blank, reminding her of those awful looks when his brain went spinning, but this blankness was different. A kind of stiffness, as if she'd offended him.

"Dev, I'm sorry." She grabbed the material of his shirt, fisting it in her hands. "I *hate* him being a part of you, being in your brain. I—"

He kissed her, taking her with his mouth and ravishing her. His warm, large hands cradled her face as he tasted and explored her. She'd never before been kissed into thoughtlessness, but his tongue had her clinging to him as his hands roamed her body, molding it so she pressed fully against him.

She emerged breathless and he backed her up to the wall, leaned into her, his erection hard against her belly, his mouth sucking on her neck.

"Where?" she asked, feeling bewildered by the sensory overload.

"Where?" he repeated, also a question, but before she could think of what she'd been meaning to ask, his mouth latched onto her cotton-covered nipple and pulled the nub into his mouth.

She moaned, arching into him, wishing there was no material between her breast and the moist heat, yet not wanting to be released either. Lust coiled deep in her belly and her pussy throbbed as blood pooled there, demanding she be released, demanding she be held tighter. Something inside her was climbing.

As if he knew exactly how she felt, he slid palms around her buttocks and raised her up, all the while sucking on her breast, the cotton now wet and slightly abrasive against her nipple. She wrapped her legs around his waist so he could move her away from the wall and carry her to the double bed.

He set her down on the mattress, lifted her tank top over her head, pushed her backwards and pulled off her shorts. She was naked; he was clothed. When she opened her mouth to point that out, he shushed her, tracing a finger over her lips. He knelt beside her. "I want you to know how beautiful you are."

Her brow creased and he said, "Yes," then trailed a finger down her clavicle so it rested momentarily in the dip at the base of her throat where her collarbones met. He sketched a line along her sternum to her bellybutton and then pubis.

"I want you inside me." She felt desperate for them to be together now.

His eyes glinted as he traced her slick folds. "I guess you do."

She jerked up to sitting and he took hold of her shoulders to push her down again. In turn, she gripped his shoulders. "No, Dev."

There was mischief in his eyes as he said, "No, what?"

She forced her way up to sitting again, but before she could undress him, he was kissing her, his one hand at the back of her neck, his other covering her breast. As he delved deeply with his tongue, she found herself falling back down, her body unwilling to fight when he made love with his mouth. Her nipple was caught between his thumb and finger, sending ripples through her belly and lower. She wondered if she could come just from these sensations.

He tamped down the kiss, but before she could say she wanted him again, he flipped her over on her belly.

"What are you doing?" she demanded.

"Exploring you." He nuzzled her shoulder, kissed along her

spine, tongue and lips caressing the line of her back. Then he positioned himself behind her, spreading her legs. He knelt, jeans still on, and gently pulled her up on all fours then back towards him, so her bare thighs rested on his knees. "Okay, Callie?"

"God, I don't know."

He traced a finger down the cleft of her butt, and she'd never realized the skin there was so sensitive. "You don't know?" he asked as two fingers slipped inside her. "You're so wet and engorged. Beautiful."

"I don't know anything when you love me like this."

"I am loving you."

"I want you too." She was pleading now, but didn't care as long as she heard the zipper coming undone.

"Good thing you do." His voice husky, his hands warm, pulling her to him so his cock pressed against her entrance. She pushed back and he responded with a full-body groan as he impaled her, filled her. She wanted him there, never to leave. Then he pulled out and entered again, and that was even better.

She rested on her elbows and whimpered while he entered her, again and again. Her legs began to shake, but she managed to hold herself together as a wave of pleasure engulfed her, the sensation intense, mindless, timeless. Instead of coming down, she came again, barely a break between orgasms. Dev's cock seemed to touch something deep inside of her, opening her up, loosening her in a way her body had never been loosened before. Just when she thought she couldn't hold herself up anymore, Dev stiffened, a deep sound tore from his chest, and he climaxed. He pulsed inside her and completely unraveled by their lovemaking, she collapsed. He made a noise, almost a sob as he wrapped arms around her and pulled her unresisting body back against him. She had never felt so soft, so pliable.

They slowly fell on their sides on the bed, Dev still holding her.

When she caught her breath, she turned in his arms. She smiled up at him, but he regarded her seriously, touched her cheek. "That wasn't quite how I meant it to go."

"I liked it."

"Oh, I liked it too. That's not what I meant." But his slight anxiety eased and he kissed her.

Despite her languor, she objected to his still being dressed. "You tell me what you meant while I take off your clothes."

With great effort—her body felt entirely boneless—she rolled them over, pushing him onto his back with her on top. He clasped her to him, to hold her still.

"I like you here," he said, and she dropped her head against him, overwhelmed by such simple words. No lover had uttered them to her and they made her chest ache, but in a good way. They breathed against each other, a kind of prayer of thanks, until she could rouse herself.

"You don't want to be naked, Dev?" She wondered if this was something left over from Scott's influence, from Scott insisting Dev was asexual. She felt the anger rise in her at that thought of Scott's invasion.

But Dev said, easily, "I want to be naked." So she pushed back to rest on her knees and skimmed his jeans and boxers off. Having had so little time to know him, she thoroughly examined his muscular calves, dusted with dark hair, his large kneecaps, his strong thighs. Everything about him fascinated her. She rested a cheek against his knee and gazed down. His brown eyes were dark and warm, which made her happy.

"It's not usually like this for me," she admitted.

He caught her hand, held it between his two. "I hope it's not uncomfortable."

She found herself gazing at the headboard, because she was embarrassed and yet she wanted to admit it to him. "I've never gotten wet like this."

"That just means you like me." He grinned when she looked at him again, but there was concern there too. "I got wet too. Pre-come," he added when she appeared puzzled. "I'll show you next time."

She grinned back, pleased by that idea—a next time. "I don't usually like male humans."

His brow creased. "Who do you usually like?"

"Not many people at all. I've kept to myself. Pumas can be solitary, but"—her voice hitched—"when I'm alone for too long, I ache for company. My puma protests, but the fact is, I need friends."

"Like your friend Trey." Dev sounded suspicious, perhaps jealous, though it was hard for Callie to interpret because she hadn't encountered anyone being jealous about her before.

"Trey is special. He's a werewolf, did I mention that?"

"Uh, no." Dev didn't like that piece of information, a wariness invaded his features.

"Do you believe me?"

He didn't answer.

"It doesn't matter. I'll show you some time."

"You'll show me what?"

"My puma self."

His gaze was serious, but there was no distaste. Not even a sense of unease. "You already did, Callie. This morning I saw the cougar, I saw *you* as cougar. Did you think I could forget something like that?"

188

"You seemed a little confused back there. I'd wondered if your memory had blacked it out."

"No." A short, emphatic denial. He smiled, a lopsided expression. "Not this time, anyway."

"I was confused too, so it was hard for me to know what you knew in the kitchen, or even how long you were there. The shift is disorienting. Cat thoughts mixed with human thoughts don't always make for a clear memory."

He brought her palm to his mouth. Kissed it. "I don't understand this shifting business at all. How can it even happen?"

"Well I don't understand this mind-control business either." She crawled up him, sliding fingers under his T-shirt and pushing it up so she could place a palm on his bare chest. "I just love being with you this way, Dev. That's one thing I know without a doubt."

He tugged at her so she lay sprawled across him, then speared a hand in her hair the way she was coming to adore, and kissed her while he grew hard beneath her belly.

"I love being with you too, babe."

She smiled and ducked her face into his throat. "I like it when you call me babe."

"Good."

She toyed with his short, soft hair and slowly lifted her face so she could see him. "I can't understand why Scott would tell you you're asexual. I don't like that he did that. Was it some kind of weird game?"

Dev didn't answer right away, but his face became shuttered. "No," he said finally. "Scott told me that to protect me. From other Minders. From being used for sex. They do that to some people. They've done it with Scott, you see, and that's why he fears it."

She kissed him all over his serious, now-drawn face and he traced a pattern on her shoulder. She wanted to ask, if they'd done it to him, to Dev, but found the words caught in her throat.

"I don't think so," answered Dev, as if he'd read her thoughts. "If it happened, I don't remember." He let out a long breath. "I know you dislike Scott, but you're mistaken if you think he doesn't care what happens to me. In his odd and perhaps misshapen way, he wants to protect me. When I say he's not all bad, there's truth there, not just Scott talking through me."

"If you're right, I'll forgive Scott a little. I know about wanting to protect. After all, I'm made to protect."

He frowned at that and her smile became apologetic.

"Is that bad, what I said?"

"Not bad," he said slowly. "What do you mean, you're 'made to protect'?"

"The puma in me. She—" As his frown deepened, she stopped. "What?"

"Why do you call the puma 'she'? Isn't she part of you? Aren't you one and the same? Or are you separate beings, somehow?" He touched her face because her gaze had slid away. "Callie?"

"Yes, of course we're one and the same." She could recognize that she was spoiling things, with all her talking. When they touched and kissed and made love, everything felt perfect. When they talked, nothing was perfect. Yet it was impossible not to talk when they were this intimate. His caresses brought the words out of her.

It was like the time she'd been gone in the desert for days

and she returned, shifted to human, and couldn't stop drinking water, even though it made her a bit sick. She was *thirsty* for this talk. She had longed to talk to someone for ages and Dev, unlike Trey, unlike Ruth even, didn't shut her down. She would try to explain herself to her lover.

She sat back and placed both hands on her naked chest. "I am a bit split at times. We, the puma and I, don't always want the same thing. We"—she still wasn't looking at him, in fact she slid off him and lay on her back, as if to get away from his careful regard—"fight for the body." She patted her heart again. Then wondered if she sounded and looked silly to him and wanted to hide.

Dev observed that Callie made an odd, shy gesture by putting an arm over her eyes.

"Hey." He propped himself up on one elbow and rubbed her belly before bringing her against him, and she curled into him. One thing for sure, she was tactile, responsive. He tried not to let it stoke his male ego too high, even if his male ego was in desperate need of bolstering after his fucked-up year. "That was hard for you to tell me, wasn't it?"

"Yes. But I'm glad I did." She spoke into his neck, and he had to concentrate to make out the soft words muffled against his skin. "You're the second person in the world I've talked to about who I really am. And the first normal."

"First normal, eh?" Dev found that weirdly reassuring though he suspected her idea of normal and his were different.

"I haven't had a lot of opportunity to say these hard things, to make them less hard to say."

"You weren't close to Trey." Part of Dev was relieved, even if it was stupid to be jealous. Still, Dev couldn't help but think he wouldn't have much chance against a werewolf. Did shapeshifters usually stick together?

Callie sighed. "I wanted to be."

Well, Dev could always count on Callie to be honest. "Trey's a fool."

She laughed. "I don't think so. Trey just doesn't have friends. He ignored me mostly, except when it came to work."

Dev pulled Callie closer, frowning at how lonely she sounded. Trey should have been a better friend. Someone should have been looking out for Callie, instead of just Callie looking out for others.

"And yet," he mused out loud, "Trey's coming here right away, simply because you called him."

"He's like that. Strong sense of duty. That's why I worked for him. I admired that in him."

"What was your work, exactly?"

She went stiff in his arms so he palmed her back, skimmed a hand over her ass, nuzzled her hair, until she relaxed again. Then he locked a fist into her hair and pulled her away from his neck to gaze at her amber eyes, pupils large in the darkness. He brushed lips over her forehead, grazed her eyelids as she lowered them.

"Your work is also difficult for you to talk about."

"Everything is difficult to talk about tonight, isn't it?" Her question was an odd mixture of grim and wry.

"I think you're right." He kissed her. "Do you trust me enough to tell me this?"

"You won't like me anymore, if I tell you what I did for Trey."

He stroked her neck, where some fine white scars lay. Someday he'd ask her about them, if he got the chance, but not yet. "Try me. Tell me what you did for Trey. I can promise I'll still like you. After all, *you* like a zombie."

"You've resisted them. You're not really a zombie," she protested.

"I am," he said quietly. "But you're changing the subject, Callie." He brushed lips against her neck, liking the way she shivered against him. "I like you. Trust me on this."

Like seemed such a mild, moderate word. Dev felt strong emotions for this girl-woman-puma in his bed, but he sure as hell wasn't going to float the word *love* tonight. Especially when he didn't know what tomorrow was going to bring, apart from pain.

"You aren't a zombie," she repeated, avoiding her topic, but also desperate to believe what she said.

He wouldn't deceive her, but he had to clench his jaw for a moment before forcing himself to speak the truth. "I am. It's a rather weak position, being under Scott's control."

"You're strong."

He appreciated the faith she had in him, but his laughter was rueful. "Callie, you've seen me at my very worst—"

"Your very best," she corrected. "You are so strong, to fight the way you have, to protect those you can. Like my sister, like Madison."

He snorted, his self-disgust rising in his throat, though he had sworn he would not get mired in his own deficiencies when he was in bed with Callie. She deserved better than that. He refused to make their last night together all about him and his inadequacies.

Her fingers brushed against his face. "I truly believe that."

His eyelids drifted to half-mast and he let out a long breath. "I was told once, long ago, that the reason Scott can control me so well is *because* of my protective instincts. They're so strong they play into what Scott wants of me." He laughed. "Of course,

Scott was a boy and he was obviously at risk. Many people would have felt and done the same."

"I'm not so sure about that." She pressed kisses against his chest, which was oddly endearing and slightly unusual. Not that they'd been together enough to understand a lot about each other's usual. Still, the act seemed to be a kind of supplication. He wasn't entirely sure what she wanted of him. Forgiveness?

"I killed my own kind," she admitted to his shoulder, then let her face fall against him.

He held her as she went still. "Go on."

"Mostly men," came her muffled voice, "though they were in cougar form. Feral. Violent. Lost." She paused. "Murderers."

"It is sometimes necessary to kill murderers." He knew that now, felt no regret for what he'd done today, even if he flinched when he thought of that moment he'd pulled the trigger. "Perhaps you've forgotten, but I killed someone this morning. Max. Shot him in the face."

She lifted her head from his chest. Gazed at him, a kind of understanding on her face. "I've killed killers, Dev, and so have you. We have that much in common."

They clung to each other then. Dev still hard and Callie so soft. He maneuvered so that he entered her. With her on top, he could finally go slow. It was a languorous lovemaking where Dev tried to show her just how much he cared.

Because tomorrow, though Callie didn't know it, they would part. If he made it out alive, he would find her again, and if he didn't, she would remember them together like this.

Chapter Sixteen

In the dark, while Callie lay sated and sleeping, Dev slipped away to Scott's room. He approached the bed grimly, stood there looking at the sleeping form with a sense of the inevitable, then reached down and shook the boy's shoulder.

Before Scott could make a sound, Dev clapped a hand over his mouth and watched Scott struggle with fear.

Dev's low murmur of "it's me" calmed the boy down and he went still. Dev removed his hand, because Scott didn't much like being touched.

"We have to keep Callie out of this. Already, she's too involved. It's dangerous for her." Dev barely spoke the words, knowing that Callie's hearing was extremely sensitive.

"Okay," Scott whispered. He gazed at Dev who tried not to flinch, but the next words did not contain a push, just a kind of dead hopelessness. "It's time to go, Dev. Go back."

"I know."

Scott closed his eyes, but whether it was relief or dread, or just a fucked-up mess of emotions Dev couldn't begin to unravel, he didn't know. Didn't want to know, at least right now. Instead, he gave the boy instructions. "We'll go in the morning. When you get up, pack your things. If you talk to her, tell her you're leaving, that you no longer want to be with us. She'll be relieved for my sake, though probably worried about

195

you."

Scott pulled a face. "Yeah, right. She hates me."

Dev shook his head but didn't argue. "Pack my things too. I left everything downstairs, including Max's gun. You *must* pack that gun. Okay?" Scott nodded. "Then you wait for me by the car. I'll join you, alone."

Callie was no doubt a fast runner, but not as fast as a car. Dev just needed to take off at the right moment, when she was momentarily distracted. She wouldn't be expecting this development, not after tonight.

The worst thing about his plan was that he would abandon her. She was too alone and somehow the knowledge that Trey was arriving here tomorrow didn't make Dev feel any better.

After Scott agreed, Dev quietly left Scott's room, used the washroom and slid back into bed with Callie. She didn't waken, but she cuddled against him, a bittersweet act from Dev's point of view. They had so little time left together, but he would take this. Despite his regrets, he tried to fall back asleep as he held her, but mostly he lay awake, soaking up her presence, and fought against thinking about what was to come.

In the morning, once dawn began to lighten the sky, Dev heard Scott moving around, preparing for their departure. Cautiously, Dev edged away from Callie, hoping to silently join Scott, perhaps take off before she was even awake. But she opened her eyes as Dev rose.

"Hey." There was question in her eyes and perhaps doubt. She was sensitive to his moods.

He tried to smile, but he wasn't sure how genuine it looked. He'd have liked to kiss her deeply, but settled for pushing hair off her brow and brushing his lips across her forehead. Then he turned away and quickly pulled on his clothes.

"What's the rush?" she asked.

"I thought you said Trey was arriving today?" he said somewhat stiffly.

She appeared puzzled and a little hurt that he was acting so distant after last night. Christ, he hated this. Then again, he'd hated the entire past year, so what was new?

"You don't approve of Trey?" So she thought this was the key to understanding Dev's demeanor this morning.

"No, that's not it. I just want to be prepared." They'd talked so much last night that Dev supposed his muted disapproval of Trey had been evident.

"Trey is a good guy. Really."

"I'm glad." At his quiet voice, she frowned, then got up and listened.

"I don't hear Scott. I think he went outside."

Dev walked over to the window that looked out onto the front yard. "He's packing the car." He left a deliberate pause. "As if he's leaving."

"Really?" She obviously hadn't expected that. "I'm surprised, given yesterday."

Dev shrugged without looking at her.

"He seems so dependant on you. Where would he go?"

Dev shook his head to indicate he didn't know. He didn't want to lie if he could help it.

"Perhaps we should talk to him." She cast Dev a look of concern. Yep. She might not like what Scott's powers had done to Dev's mind, but she was also worried about Scott's welfare.

"Perhaps," Dev allowed.

"I can't imagine him going anywhere without you. He doesn't seem to know how to function without you."

"Well, he's had a time of it."

"I know it, or I wouldn't have allowed him to come here with us in the first place."

Again, Dev shrugged and Callie gave him a once-over. He supposed his nerves were showing.

"You okay?"

"Sure." He paused, saw she was waiting for more. "It's just a lot going on, Callie. Sometimes my brain feels ready to explode. Even when Scott isn't actively pushing me."

She nodded. "Okay, I'll just duck into the bathroom and we'll go see what Scott's up to." She gave him a warning look. "Wait for me though. Don't go to him alone."

"'Kay." Dev held her gaze for a moment, and satisfied with his word, she strode down the hall and into the washroom. "I'm going to make coffee," he called as she shut the door.

He made himself walk, not run, down the stairs. As silently and quickly as possible, he opened the door to outside and loped to the car. At Dev's gesture, Scott ducked into the driver's seat.

Dev jumped in the passenger side and gave a terse, "*Go.*"

Scott gunned it, he sure wasn't quiet, backing out the short drive, shifting gears and squealing down the road.

"Don't look back, Dev," Scott suggested, but Dev, who dreaded to turn around, did just that...

...to see Callie pelting out of the house and sprinting down the street just as Scott, ignoring the stop sign, rounded the corner. She was alarmingly fast and Dev felt sick at her effort.

She was trying to rescue him from Scott's clutches.

"Faster," Dev gritted out, keeping his gaze trained on the back window. He felt he owed Callie that respect, to watch her try to reach him. If he wasn't careful, he'd tear up and he despised his own tears. Especially in these circumstances, when he was abandoning her under the guise of being pushed and taken by Scott.

By the time they made their second right-hand turn, Callie was no longer in sight. She was fast, but not that fast. Dev continued to face backwards, waiting to see if she would emerge on the main street before they hit the highway. But he didn't see her again. They reached the on-ramp and sped up.

He had betrayed her. Loved her too, yet it was the betrayal she would ultimately remember.

When he finally turned around to face forward, Scott glanced over at him. "Sorry, Dev."

"Not as sorry as I am."

Bent over, hands on knees, Callie heaved breaths near the highway. She'd never run this hard as human and she felt like throwing up. Or maybe that was because Dev was with Scott again, and she had no way in hell to find them. Her despair threatened to rise up and strangle her.

The only thing that kept her from giving up was Trey's imminent arrival. Trey was a problem solver, and he'd been very interested in, even knowledgeable about, this whole Minder business. He also had access to unusual information. He had to help her find Dev.

When she got her wind back, she straightened up and slowly made the long walk back to the "safe" house that no longer felt safe. She was shocked and confused, found it difficult to think straight. It reminded her of when she took a blow to the head and she'd felt stunned for a good day. But she didn't have time for that. She needed to figure out a way to track Dev. Puma sympathized. In fact, her cat sympathized so much that Puma wanted Callie to shift.

It was tempting, because when Callie was alone, she felt

weak. She just wanted to retreat into Puma, who loved being solo, and forget everything.

Dev had left her. She'd known that he would leave her at some point in the future when the gap between cat and normal became too great. But his departure felt brutal after last night, when he'd been so tender, when she'd told him things she'd never told anyone else. When she'd thought they were in this together.

He hadn't even said goodbye. He'd just gone to make coffee...

She gave her head a sharp shake. Yes, she felt abandoned—what was new? Her life had been a series of people leaving her, starting with her mother, ending with Dev. However, she had to look at the facts in this case. Dev had not departed on his own, but with Scott. *Scott*, who was still in Dev's brain telling him what to do, and Callie was frightened for Dev's state of mind. She feared Scott was going to inadvertently kill him, because the boy didn't seem to understand just how powerful he was, didn't seem to recognize that Dev might have a breaking point.

This was another thing Trey understood—the power of the Minders. Callie had been able to recognize that over the phone. Trey's intense interest had not come from nothing.

Though she was perhaps grasping at straws, she chose to believe Trey could help Dev.

For a half an hour, Dev sat rigid with fury. Beside him a silent, almost cringing Scott drove. The boy had screwed with Dev's mind, yes, but others had screwed with Scott, had pretty much programmed him to mess with others and, more to the point at the moment, to always return to the pod. So Scott was driving "home" and scared shitless about it.

All in all, Dev wasn't sure where to direct his rage. At himself, yes, for being sucked into this mess, but there were others he could certainly blame.

Not Scott, though. Dev would like to kill Eleanor who had ruined Scott. Minders weren't innately evil. Dev was convinced of it, could remember a timid, tenderhearted boy who had craved some adult attention.

"What do we do now?" the boy asked, darting a zillionth glance Dev's way. Scott was nervous, constantly flexing his hands on the driver's wheel.

Dev rubbed his forehead, wishing that he could reclaim his ability to think, to be clever, *smart.* He used to be, before he'd been recruited by the agency to help them flush out Minders.

Christ, focus, Dev, don't dwell on past history. "Remind me again. What was the original plan?"

Scott let out a watery sigh. "We were supposed to rescue people from the pod. I'd take Eleanor and Max's cast-offs and you'd rehabilitate them."

Right, though that was *after* Dev lost contact with the agency. What had been the plan beforehand? He tried to go back in time, though using Scott as a source of facts was problematic, for so many reasons. "When'd I start losing it?"

"Around Christmastime, things got worse." Scott's grip on the wheel turned his knuckles white. "Max came to visit then and I really had to work on you, to make you a convincing zombie, or he would've found out about us. Would have realized you were more friend than anything. But after I convinced Max, well, you never trusted me again." Scott cast Dev his mournful, resentful gaze.

Dev blew out a harsh breath. It was all too fucking convoluted and he was worried they weren't going to find their way out of this mess. Especially with Scott's compulsion to return to the pod. Dev had to delay that homecoming, and prepare.

"My memory is crap, Scott. I've got to put the pieces together before we do anything."

"Sorry." It wasn't clear what Scott was sorry for specifically so Dev just took it as a general sentiment.

"Well, I'm sorry too." Dev scrubbed his face. "Help me figure it out, okay? Maybe there's a plan we can come up with."

"Like last time?" Scott said acidly. "The plan that made you hate me?"

"I don't hate you, Scott, but if you think anyone wants to be anyone's zombie, you should know better."

"We agreed!"

"Absolutely, we agreed." Dev did remember that now. Thank God his memory was getting jogged free. Weird how much Callie had helped with that... Resolutely, Dev placed thoughts of Callie aside. "That agreement is over. No more pushing or I think my brain will fall out. Sometimes it feels like it's made of Styrofoam. Nothing there but white gunk that fills my skull. Nothing useful." Except maybe rage. He could feel the red haze washing through him. That he'd been reduced to this, this *thing* that did as others bid...

"It saved your life, Dev." Scott's voice was low, intense, defensive. Some fear too, because anger frightened Scott, even if that anger belonged to his zombie, Dev.

Dev swallowed and tried to pull himself together. Impotent fury would accomplish nothing. "I realize that. But it's over. No more pushing. No more zombie Dev, okay?"

Scott scowled, presumably at his own memories. "I didn't like pushing you because you fought too hard, and I told you not to fight. I told you—"

Dev cut him off. "How long were we supposed to do this? Rescue people, that is."

"Just until the agency raided the pod's house. You *said* it would be three months max. But they never came."

Fucking agency. They'd recruited him and left him high and dry. Dev needed details, which were alarmingly fuzzy. "'The agency'? Who the fuck are they?"

Scott gave him a look of alarm. "You used to work for them, Dev."

"I know that. I can't remember fuck-all about them."

"Horton was your contact."

Dev rolled his hand in a go-on gesture.

"You didn't like them much. Even at the beginning when you hoped they'd do something to help me."

"So what the hell was I doing with them?"

"They found you because you used to be my Big Brother, and they convinced you I was in trouble and that they wanted to help me."

"I was an idiot."

Scott stared ahead, gripping the wheel hard. "No. It wasn't hard for them to convince you I was in trouble. Because I was."

Dev remembered that, the sick feeling of a year ago when he'd discovered that Scott was being abused, Scott who he'd promised he would always help. But, "Hey, you phoned me, remember?"

"After you wrote, Dev."

"Oh." Made sense, he guessed. The agency had put him in contact with Scott.

"Anyway, unfortunately the agency was kind of incompetent. Because Eleanor pegged them right away as agents, then got access to them and forced the other agents to decide the pod was made up of just normal people. They left the pod completely alone, but you got stuck inside. With me. You still thought the agency would find you, but they didn't. End of story."

"Why didn't Eleanor peg me?" asked Dev.

"She believed your Big Brother story. Because it was true, and because you actually cared about what happened to me. She found it *ironic* that I then turned the tables on you and controlled you. She approved." Bitter words.

The old memories surged forward. It was terrifying what he'd forgotten, and if Dev had had time, he would have been flattened by them steamrolling over him. But events were barreling down on him and he had to act, not react. "So I really was your Big Brother?"

"You were. That's how the agency could search you out and hire you on, remember? You had a natural in."

"Christ." Then Dev recalled something else. "You helped me forget that."

Scott blinked over at him, looking defensive. "You told me to. You said you had to be truly zombie-like or our plan wouldn't work. Max and Eleanor wouldn't believe in you and they'd kill us both, me for being 'weak' and protecting a zombie, and you for knowing about us. So you *couldn't* know about us."

Dev grunted.

"Instead," continued Scott with brittle false cheer, "they're going to kill us now."

If only Dev could think more clearly. He gathered what he could of his thoughts and gave Scott another warning. "I don't want Eleanor to know about Callie."

"If they make us talk—"

"We'll have to be careful."

"I don't want to die, Dev."

God, Scott sounded young then, and Dev remembered the child, scarcely a teen, so frightened, so alone.

Dev gave his head a sharp shake. Too many memories were crowding in, overwhelming him. He'd spent months with a brain too empty, trying to find his thoughts, and now they were all slamming down on him. What had previously been fogged and something to shy away from were now coming through in crashing Technicolor. His head pounded, blood throbbed at his temples.

"I don't want you to die either, Scott. Let me think on this. If I can."

"I'm driving towards the pod." Scott's tone was troubled. Dev knew that it was Eleanor who would have programmed Scott to always go home. Max was dead, but Eleanor was alive and powerful. Get rid of Eleanor and Scott might be freed. Which meant Madison and Ruth and Callie would be safe. Scott couldn't know Dev planned to kill Eleanor, because Scott would feel compelled to stop Dev.

Another killing. Dev wasn't used to it, but he could do it. He could murder this woman. What had Callie said last night? That they had murder in common, the killing of killers. It wasn't exactly the way he'd wanted to bond with her. Still, here he was.

"I know where you're headed, Scott. But we'll need to stop at a hotel for the night, because I've got a migraine that is going to kill me if I don't get out of this sunlight."

Scott shot him a troubled glance. "I can drop you and go on ahead."

Dev shook his head.

"I want to, Dev. Let me go back alone. I'll say Max killed you."

"You'll tell Eleanor the truth, Scott, because you'll have to. Then they'll come hunting me, Callie, Ruth and Madison, not necessarily in that order. I have to stay with you. Fewer questions will be asked. Just, in the meantime, I need a fucking plan. So we're going to stop at a hotel." Dev looked across at Scott, wondering how strong the compulsion to return was. Surely a one-night stay at a hotel wasn't impossible. After all, Scott had spent yesterday with him and Callie, driving away from the pod, not hightailing it back to Eleanor.

Scott let out a shuddering breath. "Yes, we can stay one night. I can handle that."

"Good."

"Nothing is good."

"True, but it will have to do," Dev said dryly. "Listen, I'm going to shut my eyes and I need silence for a while, okay?"

"Yeah, okay." Scott's voice suggested nothing was okay. But Dev did close his eyes while he tried to put together a plan of escape, for him, for Scott, and for Ruth and Madison.

Chapter Seventeen

When Callie phoned Trey, she got switched to voice mail. He was probably on a plane now. That or he'd turned off his phone for other reasons.

So she waited, and waiting that afternoon out was one of the hardest things she'd ever done. Oh, she did stuff too. Showered. Paced the house. Ate as much as she could without making herself sick. Because she wanted to have energy stores in case she and Trey had to shapeshift more than once. Their bodies burned through calories at an amazing rate during those shifts.

It was late afternoon before a car pulled into the driveway and Callie flung herself out the door to see the man whose help she needed.

"Trey." His name came out almost as a hiss of relief.

He emerged from the car, briefcase in hand, then popped the trunk and grabbed a duffel bag. With long strides, he approached the front steps, acknowledging her with a brief nod. His face was grim, drawn, and he looked weary. She wondered where he'd flown from but knew better than to ask. Trey never appreciated questions.

"Let's go inside," he said.

She backed up and he passed by her, dumped the bag, but not the briefcase, and aimed straight for the kitchen. She followed.

He placed the briefcase on the kitchen table, grabbed a glass of water from the sink, and turned to her. "You're alone." It wasn't a question but an observation. Trey's sense of smell and hearing told him Callie was the only one here.

"Scott and Dev left this morning."

"Why?"

To her horror, she teared up.

He didn't become annoyed by her show of emotion, he simply pulled out a chair for her, patted the cushion and got down to business. "Sit. Tell me what's going on. I was expecting three of you. This changes things."

"I don't know what happened," she said, bringing herself under control. "I mean I do, just not *how*. Somehow Scott forced Dev to leave with him even though I kept them apart, and I thought Scott agreed to not push Dev, and Dev agreed to not visit Scott, but..." She lifted her face to meet his gaze and admitted, "They fooled me."

He gave a short shake of the head. "Don't beat yourself up. This situation is very new to you. You tried to keep a Minder and his zombie apart. These guys program their people. Dev would feel compelled to go to Scott, even if he didn't or couldn't admit it to you. Minders like control, demand it of the people who surround them."

"But Scott, he, I don't know, he seemed to *depend* on Dev."

Trey cocked his head in question. "Yeah? Elaborate."

"Scott was needy. He was almost scared to be without Dev."

"A bit odd. After all, Scott could always claim another zombie. It's not that hard for them to do, there are enough isolated people in the world. Then again..." Trey bent over the table and snapped open his briefcase, pulled out his computer, some papers. "I've done some research. Have a friend in the know. It's likely that Scott is at the bottom of the pack. Pod," he amended, with a glimmer of an ironic smile. "That's a dangerous, vulnerable place to be. Perhaps that played into his dependence on this Dev."

This Dev. No, he was *her* Dev. She'd told Trey they were lovers and he'd filed it away as just one more fact. However, this was the time to deal in facts. "You know about these people, these Minders." She tried not to sound accusing.

"I do."

"You have information on them."

"Yes," said Trey blandly. "When I stumbled upon your existence four years ago, I was there for a reason. I wasn't just the tourist I claimed to be." His words became clipped, a little angry. "I worked for an agency."

"What kind of agency?"

"Don't ask. An asshole agency. It has very recently and suddenly been disbanded, lost all credibility." Trey waved his hand, to dismiss this point. "Back then, I was here to investigate a pod of Minders. Unfortunately, I couldn't find them. Even though Ruth was supposed to lead them to me."

"*Ruth?*" Callie still couldn't get her mind wrapped around Ruth being involved, had always thought Trey's semiannual mentions of Ruth were a tepid attempt to show an interest in Callie's personal life. Apparently not. "But how? I mean, God, she was only sixteen then."

"It was thought that her band of high school friends had been contaminated by a group of Minders, and the agency was concerned." He opened his hand. "Unfortunately I could not find evidence. I had to give up."

"She sure as hell has been contaminated since. I don't even want to think about what she's been through." Callie sank her hands into her hair and curled into herself. She should have done more to protect Ruth. "Not that my sister hasn't been drawn to abusers before, but this is worse. And I didn't even know."

"Minders are good at making sure no one knows, Callie. That's their specialty. Besides, wasn't that your time in the wild?"

She acknowledged her semi-feral younger years with a nod. Puma had needed to work something out of her system while Ruth was a young teen, when Ruth was first being contaminated. Because when Sheena, their guardian and Ruth's grandmother, had died, Callie hadn't been allowed to take care of Ruth. She'd been put into a foster care, and Callie's grief at the loss of her family had come close to breaking her.

"Just be glad you're helping Ruth now. You've rescued her from Scott. She's no longer with him."

Yeah, but. Callie traced a finger over the edge of the table. "Thing is, Trey, Scott's been a dream after her nightmare with Max." The idea of Max with Ruth made Callie sick.

Trey frowned. "Scott's been a *dream*? What do you mean?"

"Well, it's not that he wasn't disturbingly controlling and that she wasn't mind-bogglingly fawning. But from what I saw, Scott used his power to force her to eat and sleep well."

"Eat and sleep well," Trey repeated slowly, disbelief in his voice. "That's all?"

"I think so."

"They didn't have sex, Scott and Ruth? Or Scott and Dev, for that matter?"

"Nope. My impression is that Scott doesn't like sex."

Trey pulled back his lips to bare his teeth, his expression one of distaste. A low growl escaped. "Let's not guess why that is."

Callie wasn't sure what all that implied, except that it wasn't good. Trey was glowering. Goodness, this was the most emotion she'd seen Trey exhibit. Well, except for the time she almost died.

He slammed the flats of his palms down on the table. "Tell me why you want to protect Scott—that's what I've been picking up from you on the phone, and here. If he's worth protecting, I need to be convinced, because these people are dangerous and not necessarily salvageable."

She shook her head, suddenly confused by Scott and her desire to shelter him. Even after he'd essentially abducted Dev this morning.

"Callie," Trey said softly. "Scott is the key here, one way or the other, so you need to explain him to me."

She pulled in a long breath and visualized the nondescript boy who had started off as the weirdest control freak she'd ever met and changed over to someone who was terrified of the now-dead Max and the still-alive Eleanor.

"He's like this young male, more dangerous than he realizes, but lost." Trey nodded encouragement and she continued. "He needs guidance, but isn't hopeless, I think. He has some idea of doing good work, or his idea of good work. Even if he goes about that in the wrong way, in a way that damages those he's supposedly helping. That said, perhaps I don't really understand him. I thought I could keep Dev away from him, and I failed. I didn't realize, or I didn't want to realize, that Dev would be compelled to go to Scott."

She glanced at Trey, wondering if that was enough. "Is this what you want to know?"

"If you think Scott isn't a lost cause, I'm willing to help him."

"Is it too risky? I wanted to save both Dev and Scott—and instead I saved no one."

Trey eyed her. "Don't give up yet. I'm going to do my best, and I have resources."

She sighed, searching his face for...what? Absolution? "I think I know what happened. I got so tired of bringing in young males for the kill. Scott is only nineteen. I couldn't face destroying him too."

"For good reason, Callie. Scott is not a feral, whatever the Minder version of feral is, or he would *not* have been taking care of your sister the way you described."

She acknowledged that with a nod. "Scott's biggest thing with Dev was having him cook."

Trey blinked. "Well I guess Scott is a bit of a homebody or something."

"Something," agreed Callie.

"From what you say, he's not hopeless. I'm going to bring him in. I have contacts who I think can control him and would be willing to help him. However, we can't lose sight of the fact Dev, by just being with Scott, is in danger now. It's not healthy, being a zombie."

"Dev's not a zombie." Even as she spoke, it no longer seemed true. Dev, after all, had gone with Scott.

Trey eyed her with something close to pity. "I doubt that very much."

Callie jerked a hand up to wave away her argument. "Can you find them?" There'd been a time when Callie had thought Trey could do everything and maybe she was expecting too much, but please God, let Trey be capable of this.

He pinned her with his cold blue gaze and she saw determination. "I can find them. In fact, I have."

Tears pricked at her eyes, and she saw Trey seize up in reaction to this second show of emotion—too much in such a short period of time—so she got hold of herself. "How? How did you find them?" She kept her voice even.

"Actually, *I* didn't find them. A friend with connections looked into it for me."

"A *friend*?" Callie didn't think Trey had friends.

The corner of Trey's mouth kicked up. "I consider him such. While I'm not sure he'd use that word to describe his relationship with me, he nevertheless owes me."

She frowned. "You couldn't identify these Minders four years ago. What's so special about your friend that he has and so quickly?" She fisted her hands. "He has to be right, Trey. We simply don't have time to fail."

"I know that, Callie."

She nodded. "Good."

"You asked what's so special? He has connections for a reason." Trey leaned forward. "Not all Minders are bad, Callie. My friend, he's a Minder too."

Callie shivered, unsure if she should take that news as good or bad. Trusting Trey made sense to her so she simply nodded as he packed up his computer again.

Not long after Trey's revelation, they hit the road. They had an address for what was apparently the pod's home base—a house in the suburbs.

"Does your friend like spying on his own kind?" Callie asked while Trey sped along the highway. Maybe it was good to know some Minders would help others. On the other hand, maybe this "friend" would turn out to be as sneaky as Scott.

"It's not spying," Trey said flatly. "It's looking out for people like himself. He's been part of a dysfunctional pod, bottom of the heap like Scott, so he's willing to help me clean this one up." Trey glanced at Callie. "He knows exactly what that entails."

She sank into her car seat. "Why does it have to be so hard?"

Trey lifted his eyebrows and it was encouragement enough for Callie to go on.

"Why do us freaks have to have such murderous kin? People we have to kill? Why do our own kind inflict such harm?" She was thinking not only of Max, but of the ferals she'd lured in for Trey's people to kill.

Trey didn't answer for at least five minutes. Callie thought he wasn't going to, that there simply wasn't an answer to her question. Finally he said, "We have to get them young and save them."

"Not easy to do."

"Well, Callie, if I ever find a young werecougar that I think can make it, I am going to count on you to raise it. And you're right, it won't be easy. It'll be the toughest job you'll ever have."

The puma in Callie seemed to leap at the suggestion. No dismay, despite her recognition that it *would* be a difficult undertaking.

"I'd like that." She realized she was speaking for both her halves. If nothing else, these god-awful few days had brought Puma and her in line. They both wanted to protect, they both wanted to love, and they both wanted to destroy those who destroyed others.

"So what exactly are we going to do now?" Puma was spoiling for a fight with Eleanor, whose Minder powers needed to be brought to an end.

"We're going to scout out the premises. Then I'm going in to execute Eleanor."

Callie swallowed. This was the stone-cold Trey she knew. It was chilling, but under the circumstances, also reassuring.

"Surely you haven't forgotten I'm a killer, Callie." The tone was flat, the irony hinted at.

"I haven't forgotten. I called you because of what you are."

Dev wasn't a killer. He wasn't even a cop. He'd been studying law till he'd dropped out last year. Criminal law, sure, and that was the reason he knew how to handle a gun. He'd thought, way back when, in the days before he'd become entrapped by the agency, that he should know about guns if he was studying cases that involved people using guns.

He glanced at the empty passenger seat. The gun glinted as he passed under the highway's bright lights. He rather dreaded pulling that trigger again. Not that he could regret Max's death, far from it. Max had been a sadistic, abusive bastard. Nevertheless, the actual killing of someone, of taking someone's life, made Dev feel rather ill.

He'd wanted to study law, not end up like this. He set his jaw, annoyed at the pang of self-pity. He'd sworn he wouldn't get maudlin and frankly he couldn't afford it right now. He'd lose his focus and any chance of success.

If he was lucky, Scott wouldn't waken till morning, and by then it would be all over. Dev had convinced Scott they should stop for the night, about an hour away from Eleanor's, and they'd pulled into a Marriott, Scott's credit card paying for their stay.

The boy hadn't been sleeping well, not since Callie had handcuffed him to the bed. So once Scott dozed off and appeared to drift into deeper sleep, Dev had very quietly picked the car keys off the desk and slipped out of the room.

The gun he had left in the car and now it was his companion.

He passed under another bright highway light. Three more exits till he hit the one he would take. As he approached it, his gut tightened a little more.

Thirty minutes later, Dev pulled off the main street and made his way into the upscale suburb. Not a safe house this time. Nothing safe about it.

This subdivision had huge houses. Clearly the pod was rich. Dev came to their court but drove past and parked the next street over. He wanted to walk up to the house and he didn't want them to take his car if he could help it.

He got out of the car with the gun, wearing a jacket to hide the weapon from sight. Nevertheless he felt like the gun was lit up in neon and everyone could see it. Obviously he was not the kind of person who relaxed while wearing a weapon. He inwardly rolled his eyes at himself. As if he could relax tonight no matter what he carried.

So he took a few minutes to get used to the idea that he was walking up to Eleanor, with a gun. He locked the door, then spent a moment leaning against the car, arms resting on top, while he got his head together for this one final act. His biggest fear was that his brain was so zombie-stupid that what seemed like logical action from inside it, with at least a chance at succeeding, would actually turn out to be pure idiocy.

He'd probably never know and there simply wasn't time for second-guessing. Scott would be heading this way, possibly now, definitely by tomorrow. Dev could not allow Eleanor to get hold of Scott. Not only would she set him up for further abuse, she'd find out about Madison and Ruth, and for that matter, Ian and Helen.

Even Callie.

Dev couldn't allow it. He had to kill Eleanor, before she opened her mouth.

With that thought, he pushed away from the car and started walking. His favorite scenario had Eleanor opening the front door and Dev putting a bullet in her head. Once she was dead, Scott could no longer return to her, and he wasn't bound to anyone else in the pod. If Dev could intercept him before another Minder got his claws in, Scott could go free.

However appealing this scenario, Eleanor was unlikely to open the door. She didn't do things like that. Evidently for good reason, Dev thought grimly. So Dev would go to the door, act like he was Scott's zombie and be completely distressed because Scott was in big trouble. The Minder who greeted him would then take him to Eleanor.

At least it wouldn't be hard to act distressed. Because he sure as fuck was.

Things might play out differently, more violently. He might have to kill Minders other than Eleanor in self-defense, though he disliked the idea of being their judge and executioner. He had gone into law for a reason, had believed everyone deserved due process. But these Minders were outside the law and their words were lethal. For that matter, they might push him the moment they saw him and he'd be dead in the water.

By a very thin thread, he hung on to the fact that Minders had a policy about not encroaching on each other's property. Dev officially belonged to Scott.

Of course, Scott belonged to Eleanor.

Still, he thought, mustering *some* optimism, there was enough to make this plan work. He had to believe that. Eleanor couldn't know that Dev was prepared to kill her, given that she thought she held tight control over Scott.

The agency, the fucking agency, had promised to swoop in

and save not only him, but Scott and any other innocents. What a fucking joke. The rage boiled within Dev and gave him the energy to walk faster, reach his destination more quickly.

Later on, he would never remember those ten minutes it took for him to walk from the car to the house. One moment he was at the car, trying to clear his head, the next, he was standing at the front door. He didn't allow himself to hesitate or he'd freeze up. He raised his fist and rapped on the painted wood.

Chapter Eighteen

The seconds stretched out and his mind seemed to empty. He allowed his thoughts to scatter, his face to become vacant. After all, he needed to act like a zombie and that just wasn't much of stretch, given the way he'd spent this past year.

A stranger opened the door. A Minder he hadn't met before—around his age, brown hair and blue eyed. Taller though. *Don't look into the eyes.* Dev slid his gaze over to the man's shoulder.

"I'm Scott's," he put in quickly, identifying who he belonged to, hopefully convincing this man to leave his brain alone.

"Scott's not here."

"I know." Dev dragged in a deep breath, because his next words were more difficult to say than he'd thought. "I'm here to see Eleanor."

"Why?" The man sounded a little...bored.

"I have a message from Scott. He said I could only deliver it to Eleanor." There. The man couldn't argue with a zombie doing as his Minder bid.

"All right." He reached for Dev who jolted back.

The stranger's lips twisted into a semblance of a smile. "What's your name?"

"Dev," he answered cautiously.

"I have to pat you down, Dev."

"I have Scott's gun," Dev said immediately, trying to avoid suspicion even while his heart sank. He was going to lose his weapon, which made killing Eleanor that much harder. The man held out his hand and Dev passed the gun to him. "Scott wanted me to have it, I don't know why."

The man shrugged, searched Dev for other weapons, then beckoned Dev in. He led Dev to the living room and pointed to the couch.

"Sit there and don't move until Eleanor gives you further orders." Dev startled at the push, his mind rebelling.

"Did you hear me?" the stranger asked quietly, and Dev nodded as his feet took him to the couch. In confusion, he sat, feeling fearful until he recalled he *was* here to see Eleanor. So he would wait. He certainly didn't have anything else to do. Dev braced himself for more orders from the stranger, but after eyeing Dev for a moment, he seemed satisfied and left Dev alone.

A sick feeling wound through him. Eleanor was going to arrive, ask him questions and he was going to answer every single one of them. Part of Dev wanted to rise, to leave, but such action seemed hopeless. The word *failure* echoed in his empty brain and he gritted his teeth. There had to be something he could do.

So he went to work with what he had, which wasn't much. He tried to fill his brain back up with Dev thoughts. They were there, even if hard to pin down at times. Elusive, but not impossible to find. It seemed to take forever, but at last he forced his gaze to rest upon a porcelain vase that held five pink roses. *Pretty.* More than that. *Breakable.* While Dev couldn't bring himself to move—Eleanor was not yet here to give him orders—he visualized his hand taking hold of that vase and smashing it in order to create a shard that could slice into human flesh. Eleanor's human flesh.

Hours passed, or so it felt to Dev. After a while, he remembered how Eleanor liked to forbid a zombie to move and leave them on their own, in their moldering brain, so that when she arrived, they were anxious for her to tell them something, anything, to do. But still he sat.

More time passed and all Dev could do was focus on that vase and its contents, imagining the flowers scattered, the vase shattered. Not the most powerful idea ever, but at least Dev knew the idea of breaking that porcelain belonged to him and no one else. In his mind's eye, he picked up the vase again and created a weapon.

Dev was barely aware of the car's arrival. The car door slammed, and that noise jerked him awake. He turned his head, but he didn't rise as he gazed out the front window to observe a taxi in the driveway, its top light shining in the dark as it slowly backed away. Footsteps sounded heavy on the stairs. It took a few minutes before the front door actually opened, as if the visitor was waiting for something, or someone.

The door shut again, but from the couch, Dev couldn't yet see who it was. Then three steps into the house, and Scott came into view, meeting Dev's stare with a wince and a hangdog expression. Shame and so much else passed over Scott's features. Too many emotions for one teenager. The boy looked sick. He didn't even say hello to Dev.

Instead he shifted to face the stairs leading up to the second floor and called, quite timidly, voice thin and reedy, "Eleanor?"

They waited in silence, he and Dev, until the blue-eyed stranger reappeared, jogging down the stairs. Presumably this man was Eleanor's equivalent of a butler.

"She's been waiting for you," he told Scott, whose only response was to hang his head more. "Go sit in the living room with your zombie." Scott's body jerked a little and Dev thought, *He's been pushed.* "Don't talk. Don't move."

Scott, of course, obeyed. To the letter, as he seated himself stiffly beside Dev on the couch.

Dev offered him a half-smile. "I wasn't told not to talk."

Scott's glassy gaze met Dev's, and he couldn't help but think he was in bad shape if "his" Minder was worse off than himself, a zombie. Dev should have been more dismayed by the situation, by the fact that Scott was here when Dev had tried to ensure Scott wouldn't see Eleanor ever again.

Instead Dev stared at that vase. If he reached out his hand, he could touch its neck, curl fingers around the porcelain and swing it down against the glass table.

Not yet. Wait till Eleanor gives you the orders.

It didn't take long for Eleanor to descend now that Scott was here. Her butler, an apparently obedient soul, followed behind. Eleanor was a middle-aged woman who looked bizarrely congenial. Dev could imagine that she fooled everyone who came looking for psycho Minders. She might have been an elementary-school teacher, or a matronly nurse making sure you took your painkillers after minor surgery. She even smiled in greeting as she approached them.

Dev struggled to keep up his guard and it wasn't easy.

"Where have you been, Scott?" An outsider might have thought this mild-mannered question was gentle curiosity, but it had Scott wringing his hands.

"I'm sorry, I'm sorry." His weeping began immediately and it appalled Dev afresh, the loss and the fear in that sound.

Though it wasn't the first time he had witnessed this kind of scene.

"Where's Max?" asked Eleanor in a friendly way, as if Scott weren't crying, as if Scott were a friend. "I haven't heard from him, which is highly unusual. Max is always careful to keep in touch with me. Unlike you, my dear."

Scott rubbed his eyes. Once. Twice. His breath hitched, but no words came out.

Eleanor regarded the boy steadily, her expression now one of companionable concern. "I asked you a question, Scott. You *will* answer it this time. Where is Max?"

Scott gulped air, then blurted out, "Max is *dead.*" The breathless, terrified voice made Dev angry. A red haze began washing over him, but Eleanor must not know how angry he was. It was forbidden and therefore unsafe.

"Dead?" Eleanor sounded doubtful. She even shook her head to indicate someone had made a mistake, got their facts wrong. "I find that hard to believe. Dev?" she said, facing him. He jerked his head up to meet her gaze. That was one of her rules. Meet her gaze so Dev did. "Where is Max?"

He blinked once and while a part of him wanted to shut up, to just not speak, Eleanor deserved to know the truth. Dev wanted to tell her, her gray gaze said as much.

"I shot him in the mouth," Dev said baldly. "Max bled out on the floor. Bit of a mess," he added unnecessarily.

Eleanor's eyes widened and she went a little pale, which was kind of strange given that Eleanor was never discomposed. Never. She stared at him a good long time, assessingly, then spoke very quietly. "Now, why would you shoot Max, Dev?"

Dev searched for an answer. Callie came to mind, and Puma, but he set her aside. He could not speak of Callie here. She was too precious. But Eleanor, Eleanor *needed* an answer,

223

and he was taking too long to provide one. He licked his lips and mumbled, "I wanted to."

"My, you are evasive, and unclear. I don't approve." She shifted her gaze back to Scott. "You've lost control of your zombie, Scott. You will have to kill him."

Scott pulled in a long, shaky breath and began to nod before the weeping took him again. Dev closed his eyes and then he remembered, in his mind's eye that belonged to him, the vase. Within reach. However...

Wait for Eleanor, he reminded himself. *Wait for her orders.*

"Scott." She said his name like a whip and Dev opened his eyes to see Scott twitch in reaction. "Tell Dev what he has to do."

Dev faced him, ready for orders. Then Scott did this very strange thing. He lifted his hand to his own throat and grabbed hold, like he might hurt himself. Dev felt baffled by the action.

"Stop that," Eleanor snapped, her voice sharp. "Take your hand off yourself."

Instantly, Scott's hand dropped and, worried about the boy, Dev thought of the vase again, stared at it, though he was under Eleanor's orders, and she'd said nothing of the vase.

He still wanted to break it. He focused on this desire to break it.

"Scott," said Eleanor as if she were speaking to a very dim child. "You must—"

On a sob, Scott slammed his head down on the table, hard enough that it cracked the glass, and he slid to the floor.

"Jesus," said the butler, awe in his voice. "I've never seen *that* before."

"Quiet," demanded Eleanor as she regarded Scott's slumped form. Her face gave nothing away, but Dev recognized that she was uneasy, and that meant she was even more unpredictable than usual. She bent down to look more closely at Scott.

And Dev knew. If he didn't lift his hand, force himself to reach for that vase, Scott was going to die. Dev should have waited for Eleanor's orders, he truly believed that, but he was first and foremost responsible for taking care of Scott. From beginning to end, he was Scott's protector.

In one movement, Dev rose from the couch, grabbed the porcelain vase and swung it in an arc through the air, water and flowers flying. Eleanor turned her face up towards him. "St—" The vase smashed into her mouth, breaking apart on teeth and bone.

A large, jagged shard was left in Dev's hand, and it became his only weapon and his one chance. He jammed it into Eleanor's throat, hoping for blood, or at least to slice open her voice box so she'd never talk again. *It was too late to wait for orders*, he thought, as skin and tendon gave way against the sharp edge of his weapon.

After one final push, Dev let go. Eleanor attempted to reach for the piece of porcelain, in a futile attempt to pull it out of her neck. But blood spurted, her fingers slipped and fumbled before her arm fell away, and she collapsed.

Time seemed to stand still. Suspended. Then...

"Thank you." The sincere voice came out of nowhere, or so it felt, for there was a roaring in Dev's head as time moved forward again. He couldn't see anything except Eleanor's bleeding body and the blue shard sticking out of her neck. There would be no more orders. Dev shuddered and should have felt relieved. Instead he was strangely numb, slightly out-of-body, unsure where he was, who he was with. The voice came again. "Look at me."

Dev raised his face to stare at the butler, whose large blue eyes mesmerized him. Perhaps this man could help.

"Thank you, Dev."

He frowned, trying to remember what he was being thanked for.

"Now," continued the butler, "I want you to call nine-one-one and tell the police you just murdered this poor woman. It's important you do that right away." Those eyes bored into Dev as he realized this death had to be reported to the authorities. After all, Dev wanted to be a lawyer. He believed in the police doing their job. So when the butler pointed to a side table where a phone lay, where the vase used to sit, Dev wanted to pick it up. Even if he couldn't move quite yet.

"Nine-one-one, Dev," the butler repeated. "Dial those numbers now."

Callie prowled through the ravine. During the ride over, she'd studied this area on Trey's laptop. He'd downloaded Google maps and the detail they gave was really quite incredible. Slowly she made her way up the steep bank that led to the back of the house that contained a dangerous Minder named Eleanor.

Trey was wolf beside her. After so many months, there was once again their particular animal bond. A bond she had yearned for, until she'd met Dev. It was something to shift forms with another and to travel as puma and wolf. *That* was what had drawn her so strongly to her ex-boss. She'd thought she was in love, but it had been loneliness and a rare, but shared, ability. She might never shift *with* Dev, but she could *be* with him. He gave her love and a sense of belonging.

He wanted her.

Trey, well, Trey wanted to help her when she needed him

and wanted her help when necessary. He had only ever been her friend, and a distant one at that.

This wasn't the time to think relationships. Callie focused back on the here and now, where they had to help Dev and Scott and anyone else who'd become victim to Eleanor and her pod.

"These Minders," Trey had said, "don't know about shapeshifters and our resistance to their pushes. Better to keep it that way."

So they were crawling up the side of a ravine—which was densely inhabited by bush, plants and trees—as cougar and wolf, scouting out the pod's home base. Between Trey's sense of smell and Callie's sight, and both their hearing, they'd be able to understand just who was there and perhaps where people were located in the house. Trey wanted the kill to be as clean and quiet as possible. No confrontation, just death.

They approached the house slowly and Trey, with his superior sense of smell, stiffened first. Callie lifted her head to breathe through her open mouth, and identified Dev. She also identified the awful smell of death and blood. Trey growled, low in his throat, but Callie didn't stop to decipher the wolf's meaning. The time for planning was past. Violence and confrontation had already begun. Dev was at risk. So she ran, bounding towards the house, and leapt, aiming for the screened window.

Chapter Nineteen

She flew through the wire mesh, breaking it, and landed on linoleum to skid across the kitchen floor and slam into the wall with her shoulder. The stench of death washed over her. Fear for Dev followed closely on its heels.

"What the hell was that?" came an unfamiliar voice. Then a command, as if he expected complete obedience: "Don't move, either of you."

By the time Callie righted herself, she was looking up into the face of a stranger who appeared stunned by the presence of a cougar in his kitchen. As he processed what he saw, his expression changed from that of disbelief to terror.

She hissed and the stranger scrambled backwards. They entered the living room. In a glance, she took it in—dead woman bleeding out, Scott sitting on the floor looking both bleary and weepy. Dev standing, wild eyed, pale, *pushed*.

She was ready to kill someone.

"God, Callie." Dev sounded distraught, and baffled. "You're *here*? But you shouldn't have come. Not here. Never here." He blinked at her then lifted his hand to indicate he held a phone, stared at it as if its existence baffled him. "You shouldn't have come," he repeated, blinking at the phone now. "Just, I have to make a call, okay?"

Scott lurched towards Dev. "*No.* Don't—"

"Shut up, Scott," snapped the stranger and, snarling, Callie clamped down on his leg. He screamed and she released him, leaving him to clutch his leg while he fell to the ground. Maybe *he* would shut up if he had a damaged leg. He was lucky she hadn't torn the muscle open, just punctured it.

She wasn't sure why but Scott stumbled into Dev, grabbed his wrist and shook the phone out of his hand. Dev let the phone fall.

Then Scott stomped on the phone, or tried to. He fell over on his second attempt, as if he were drunk or something, but she didn't smell alcohol. However, since Scott wanted the phone destroyed, Callie obliged him—she knew enough about Minders and their pushes. Picking up the phone in her mouth, she crunched it dead. If Dev actually needed to make a phone call, rather than being pushed to make one, it would have to wait.

"Dev," began the stranger, voice full of pain but determined. Callie turned and bit down on his leg again. It was going to be in shreds if he kept this up, but she found it hard to care even as the stranger screamed in pain again. Surely twice would teach him? She let go, he stopped yelling and she eyed him, waiting for his next move. This time he dragged himself out of the room, his ragged whimpering accompanying him. Normally, noises of pain upset her, but not now. All she wanted was this stranger to stay away from Dev, and Scott who seemed to be hurt.

Next thing she knew, Dev was sinking down beside her. His arms came around her shoulders in a hard hug. His face pressed against her neck and he simply breathed.

"I can't keep this up, Callie," Dev said in a fractured, bewildered voice. "I'm really losing it this time. Where's the phone?" He lifted one arm from her and reached for the broken phone. Gently, she caught his hand in her mouth, stopping him, then licked the nasty cut. Somehow he'd sliced his palm open.

With that, he gave up trying to retrieve the phone, just rested against her as if it was the most he could accomplish, while she licked him and purred. "Everything's red when I'm angry," he murmured, "but I'm not angry now. Not with you."

She chirped in reassurance, wishing she could tell him it would be all right, that it was over. He didn't seem to know it, even though that had to be Eleanor dead on the floor. Callie chirped again.

"I don't know what that noise means," he told her, "but it's charming."

She nuzzled his shoulder.

More footsteps and both Callie and Dev stiffened, only to see Trey emerge from the kitchen into the living room. Dev gripped her more tightly.

"We want to get the fuck out of here," Trey announced after a quick sweep of the room. "No sense in explaining this death when we can just disappear. Who else is in the house?" He looked at Scott, who sat on the floor, glassy-eyed, unable at this point to take any of it in. "What's wrong with him? He's got an egg growing on his forehead." He reached down to look at Scott's eyes and the boy flinched. Probably because Trey was a very large naked man Scott had never before met.

Dev lifted his head from Callie, spoke over her to Trey. "Scott didn't want to kill me so he knocked himself out."

"Jesus Christ." The disgust in Trey's voice was palpable.

"That made me angry," Dev muttered in Callie's ear, though Trey with his sensitive ears heard it too.

"I can imagine," Trey responded. "Okay, who else is in the house right now?"

"A butler," said Dev.

Trey stared, not making sense of Dev's information, and Callie wished she were human and could speak.

"Never mind," said Trey. "I'll figure out what to do with him later. For now, to the car. Where I can get dressed and retrieve my gun, and we can all leave."

Somehow they managed to get Dev and Scott out of the house. They hid in the shadows while Trey ran to the car and drove it back, then they piled in. Puma sat in the back, lying half across Dev's lap while he kept his arm on her like he wouldn't let go. Scott huddled in the passenger seat, and Trey reminded Scott not to fall asleep since he might have a concussion. Scott stared at him with something that lay between terror and awe, because Trey had mentioned he was a werewolf and Callie a cat shifter.

The rest of the night, as they headed back to the safe house, went by in a blur. They were all kind of stunned, not just concussed Scott. Dev, protective of Scott as ever, kept wanting to explain that Scott hadn't pushed him to leave this morning, that it had been Dev's own will. Since Callie chose not to shift in a moving car, she simply purred as soothingly as possible. She would keep her counsel here, at least for the time being, because she didn't think Dev *could* know if it had been his own will, which had been so dangerously intertwined with Scott's will this past year.

Still, there could be no doubt Scott had tried to save Dev from himself. For that, Callie forgave a lot. Not enough to allow Scott to stay with Dev, mind you. Trey had stated that a zombie and Minder needed to be separated and she wholeheartedly concurred. Trey had contacts who might be willing to rehabilitate Scott, and he deserved that second chance.

"Callie," Dev murmured. "My hand is healing."

She grinned her cat grin, though she couldn't explain the potent healing agents in her saliva.

"Now, I just have to heal my brain. If it doesn't fall out first."

She turned to face him, looked into those dark eyes that no longer seemed quite so clouded with confusion. He was a strong man, stronger than he knew, Trey had said, to have lived through this.

That conversation was for a later date. For now, she just chirped again and Dev's chest rumbled in laughter, as if her noises pleased him. "*Still* don't know what that means, but I like it."

"It means she likes you," Trey offered wryly.

Dev didn't acknowledge Trey, he just smiled at her and mouthed, "Good. I like you too."

Epilogue

"Madison! Supper!" Dev yelled.

If Madison didn't hear his call, Callie of the exceptional ears would. They were out in the backwoods somewhere, probably climbing trees.

By the time they got in, washed their hands and sat down, the homemade pizza was getting cold. No one seemed to care, least of all Dev. There was a happiness in him that hadn't existed for well over a year and he was never going to take normal for granted again.

He kissed Callie then Madison before he sat himself.

"I get to go to school tomorrow." The words were bright, excited, and Madison was obviously nervous. Well, that was to be expected.

It had been a bit of a challenge to get his guardianship of Madison established, but that process had been helped along with some gentle Minder involvement. He had mixed feelings about using mind control, even for good, but when the alternative was Madison being shunted into the foster care system, he'd decided that the means justified the ends.

Madison had gone through enough in her short life, with missing, probably dead parents, and living however briefly with Max. Now she needed stability.

So in this case, Scott had done good. Scott was doing well too. Apparently. Dev and he no longer had direct contact, for everyone's sake, said Trey, but Dev recognized mostly for his own. And if he was honest, it was a pure relief.

"Well"—Callie's voice brought him back to the present— "Dev starts school in four months." She spoke encouragingly, as if Madison and Dev were in the same boat.

And yes, Dev was going back to finish law school. He'd had the wherewithal to take a leave last year.

"What about you, Callie, will you go to school?" Madison asked.

"I don't think so, honey. I don't do well at school."

"Ruth likes waitressing, maybe you can waitress with her." Madison's earnest face made Callie smile.

"I don't like waitressing much either." Callie glanced at the clock. "Where is my sister, anyway?"

On cue, the front door slammed open and Ruth yelled, "I'm home."

"Come eat supper," Callie called back.

She arrived in the kitchen and Callie breathed in through her mouth, just to check there was no smell of cigarettes, of alcohol. She knew it was good that Ruth was working. Doing nothing had always got her sister in trouble, but she also worried about what Ruth could get up to in the outside world.

"Sure, I'll have a piece." Ruth settled down, shooting a glance at Dev. There were still shadows behind her eyes, and Dev and Ruth had struggled a little to get used to each other post-Scott, but the family life seemed to suit them both. Well, suit them all.

"We're just talking about school," Dev offered.

Ruth grinned at Madison. "Hey, kiddo, tomorrow's your big

day."

Madison lifted her chin. "Yes."

"I'll be starting school too. Online." Ruth's mouth twisted. "Going to finish high school, like I should have long ago."

Callie squeezed Ruth's shoulder. "Now's a good time, sis."

"Absolutely." In truth, Dev thought it was great Ruth had a focus.

"Big-time lawyer," said Ruth, but there was affection there, not resentment.

"Not yet," Dev pointed out.

"What are you going to be, Ruth?" asked Madison.

"Well, I've been thinking about that, but I don't really know." Ruth shrugged as if it didn't matter, but Callie knew her sister still felt rather lost. Callie also felt there was time to figure such things out. "What are you going to be, Mad?"

"A lawyer. Like Dev." Madison stared up at her guardian with shining eyes.

"Excellent," declared Dev. As Madison bit into her pizza, he shot Callie a look of sheepish amusement, and she grinned back. Any child emulating Dev was going to be fine as far as Callie was concerned.

"They're doing it again," said Madison after she swallowed.

"I know." Ruth's tone suggested she and Madison were conspirators.

"Doing what?" Callie demanded.

"Making googly eyes at each other." The smirk on Madison's face was priceless.

"*I* do not make *googly* eyes." Dev shook his head to emphasize the fact. "I don't even know what it means."

Madison's expression became sly. "It means you're getting

married."

Hell. Callie choked on her pizza and began coughing till she couldn't breathe. Ruth banged her on the back, and Madison climbed down off her chair to join in by hitting Callie's kidney with her small hand.

When she recovered, Dev was gazing at her with his knowing half-smile. "Bit of a shock there, was it, Callie? Don't worry, I didn't know about the connection between googly eyes and marriage either. Perhaps Ruth can fill us in."

Ruth held up a hand in surrender while Callie glared at Dev because her face was heating up and she didn't know what to do with her embarrassment. Truth was, they'd actually discussed marriage once, and she'd told him it was too soon. Still she cherished the conversation, and the fact that Dev seemed committed to this—Madison, Ruth, Callie, *family.*

Because family was important to Dev. He had even begun the rather painful process of ending his estrangement with his parents. Right now it was limited to phone calls, because they had too many questions he couldn't answer. And they were badly hurt by his sudden withdrawal last year. But Dev believed the breach would be healed, with time.

And belief was a wonderful thing. Callie glanced around the table at the three of them, taking in their presence and the love she felt for them. Perhaps she could believe, after all they'd been through, that it was the end of people leaving her.

About the Author

Jorrie Spencer has written for more years than she can remember. Her latest writing passion is romance and shapeshifters. She lives with her husband and two children in Canada and is thrilled to be published with Samhain.

To learn more about Jorrie Spencer please visit www.jorriespencer.com. Send an email to Jorrie Spencer at jorriespencer@gmail.com. She also writes as Joely Skye (www.joelyskye.com).

For longer than she can remember, Veronica has been wolf.
Dreams give her a name and the image of a brother.
Memory gives her nothing and no one.

The Strength of the Wolf
© 2007 Jorrie Spencer

One late winter day, David Hardway saves a malnourished wolf from a trap and takes her in. During her time with David, the wolf finds in herself the desire to be human again.

David loves the wolf he saved, but dislikes the strange woman who asks for his help. Still, he is incapable of turning away someone in need and, despite himself, David becomes intrigued. As Veronica strives to remember why she abandoned humanity for wolfdom, David becomes determined to save her from her violent past.

But others are in danger and Veronica will have to act to protect her newfound pack.

Warning: This title contains explicit sex.

Available now in ebook and print from Samhain Publishing.

hot stuff

Discover Samhain!

THE HOTTEST NEW PUBLISHER ON THE PLANET

Romance, fantasy, mystery, thriller, mainstream and
more—Samhain has more selection, hotter authors, and
everything's available in both ebook and print.

Pick your favorite, sit back, and enjoy the ride!
Hot stuff indeed.

WWW.SAMHAINPUBLISHING.COM

GREAT cheap fun

Discover eBooks!

THE FASTEST WAY TO GET THE HOTTEST NAMES

Get your favorite authors on your favorite reader, long before they're
out in print! Ebooks from Samhain go wherever you go, and work with
whatever you carry—Palm, PDF, Mobi, and more.

WWW.SAMHAINPUBLISHING.COM